A PLA

AND WOMEN

Riley Michael Parker

Lazy Fascist Press
Portland, OR

LAZY FASCIST PRESS
AN IMPRINT OF ERASERHEAD PRESS
205 NE BRYANT STREET
PORTLAND, OR 97211

WWW.LAZYFASCIST.COM

ISBN: 1-936383-94-2

A PLAGUE OF WOLVES AND WOMEN

A NOVEL

for
Gingey Mingey

still life photography

In the summer before I was banished, one of the neighbor boys died, a Nicholas I believe, a year or two younger than me and so not really a part of my life. I knew all the boys my age, and all of the older ones, but the younger children were nothing more than background noise to me, just talking furniture, as I'm sure I was to so many others. Our mothers were friends, this dead boy's and mine—my mother was friends with everyone—and so I was asked to pose for a picture with him before they had him buried. I remember that they said he had died from some sort of spell, a dizziness or a wave of heat, but when I was next to his body there was a bruising on his neck and a redness to his eyes that told a different story. They had the boy dressed in fine clothes, clothing he had likely never had a reason to wear before his death, and he was propped up on the couch, his hands folded in his lap. I was supposed to sit just as he sat, and look where he looked, as if we were reacting together.

I did as I was told.

I was not the only child asked to pose, and one of the other boys, my friend Matthew, told me that in his picture the dead boy's mouth was left open, that he was told by the photographer to laugh at the child as if he had just told a joke, as if it were a candid moment, but later, when I saw the picture, I saw that Matthew was posed just as I had been, next to the dead child, mimicking him.

On the night that I was cast out of the village, the same neighbor woman, the dead child's mother, was in attendance, standing next to my father, and I could see, even from a distance, that this woman held the picture I had taken with her son. For a brief moment, as foolish as it was, I pretended that it was perhaps to honor me along with her deceased child, but then I accepted that she had brought it to add to the fire, to burn it with everything else that I had touched or been a part of. I watched her as she tossed it into the flames, watched her face to see if she felt any sadness in losing one of the last photographs her son was ever in, but no, nothing. Her face was as solid as a tree trunk.

like the leaves in autumn

Women started losing their teeth, falling from their mouths like rotten fruit, and their hair was soon to follow. It would strike a woman suddenly, always in public, a sudden urge to run her fingers through her hair, and then when she did the hair would come out in clumps, long strands that she could hold before her; that she could marvel at; that she could grieve for. Women began to stay home, afraid that if they left their houses they would lose all of their hair, and for most women this was the case. As soon as they were out of their homes, when a man who was not their husband would look upon them, they would run their fingers through their hair and it would fall from their heads like rain to the earth.

The priest was dragged out of his house by these new creatures, these hairless and toothless hags, and called upon for answers, but he knew nothing. The gods had stopped talking to the tall man with the thin white hair long before the women had become so ugly. These beasts beat him to within an inch of his life and then carried the tattered man back into his home, lay him on the floor, and placed his mattress on top of him, hoping that he might suffocate, but the priest survived this attack, somewhat against his own will.

At the next service, church attendance was at an all-time low.

the siren

But before that there was the crying. Late at night, every night, from the center of town, we could all hear a woman crying. No one ever saw her, but we all agreed that she sounded like a pretty woman—not beautiful but somewhat intriguing, a woman with brownish red hair, fair skin, and freckles. She sounded like the kind of woman who is very self-aware, the kind of woman who spends a lot of time thinking about the universe and how she fits into it. She sounded like the kind of woman you only get one chance with, two if you're lucky, and then she's gone forever. And every night, we heard her crying.

She was a siren, we decided. Men would leave their homes, leave their wives, their children, and look for this woman. Every man claimed, as they bumped into each other in the streets, that they wanted to help this poor girl, but their eyes betrayed the lust in their hearts, the desire pumping through their veins. Us boys would leave as well, even some of the young ones, looking for this woman, most of us following throbbing erections, guided by her constant sobbing, but then we would find the voice, would be surrounded by it, and there would be no woman, just our fathers and our neighbors, embarrassed, frustrated, angry at the world, and then us boys would get beaten for leaving the house and sent back to bed. What our fathers would do after that, we had no idea.

Night after night this would happen.

Night, after night, after night.

something for everybody

The milk turned sour and the crops all died, and no rain fell, never mind the constant cloud cover. Such things were expected, but they had taken so long to go into effect that we had almost forgotten them. The few women with teeth and hair stopped sleeping and eating, so they became thin and sickly with sunken eyes. All the bald ones got pregnant, but no one knew how. No one had been sleeping with them, and no one had any plans to.

It was the married women, we realized, who lost their hair, and the single women who lost their appetite. The widowed and divorced just woke up dead, having suffocated in their sleep, drowned in their own saliva. People tried to ask the priest about it, but he had barricaded his doors and windows by that point, uninterested in watching the world around him shrivel and decay, so, naturally, his house was lit on fire. No one stayed to watch what happened, and no one ever went back to check. He had been dead to the town for quite some time.

Our fathers, surprisingly, stayed healthy. We all kept waiting for something to happen to them, for these men to deteriorate like our mothers had, but instead they got better. The grey, for example, grew out of my father's beard, and he lost the little bit of weight he had always carried around his middle then muscles developed to replace it, his loose skin now firm and taut. All the fathers were this way. This was their punishment, we realized, to get better as the women they loved got worse and worse.

And our punishment, so it seemed, as children, was to stay young and soft and sexually desirable.

As long as they could, our fathers kept away from us.

second-hand religion

Who chose who we should worship? Everyone started to ask this question, but no one knew how to answer it. The priest was already killed by then, and after the fire the nuns had gone into hiding. The choir we had seen in church each week was made of children, and none of them knew why we worshipped, just that we worshipped, and most of them had disappeared by then as well.

Our faith did not protect us or bring us comfort.

We had been raised, all of us, to worship the father of the owls, and the son of the sun, and neither of them were helping us. We had worshipped the water, and the ground beneath our feet. We worshipped the cats that lived in the trees all around us, these holy beasts watching the village with wide, alert eyes.

And then it came out that no one had seen the owls

for ages, and we all knew that the sun never came out anymore, hidden behind thick, dark, electrically charged clouds. The water became salty and unfit to drink, and the land dried up, supporting no life whatsoever, and the cats all dropped dead, their corpses dry, without blood, their bodies shriveled up like carved apples that had been left out in the summer heat.

"Perhaps," one woman said at a town hall meeting, bald, toothless, two months pregnant, "we should have worshipped the wolves."

She was right, the entire village knew that she was right, but it didn't stop them from stoning her to death for saying such a thing out loud.

the wolves

It had been the wolves, months before, that gave us the curse to begin with. They had been acting up for several years at that point—stealing livestock, breaking into the homes of the villagers, raping men's wives and daughters in the early mornings as the men tended to their crops—but they had never entered the town while the sun was up, and had never been known to move together.

My younger sister, Isobel, was the first to notice them, riding down from the mountains on the backs of ash colored bears, their own fur as black as night. She had run straight to the church when she saw them, not to our parents, not to the neighbors, and later, when questioned, she said it was for fear of me that she ran, for fear that I would stop her from warning the others. It was clear to everyone that the wolves had wanted to be seen, as they moved slow like the sun, and there was nothing that I could have done to interfere, but still, the words had been spoken.

The priest came to our home with his choir and the nuns, as our land was the closest to the forest, which meant that we were the closest to the mountains, which meant that the beasts would be passing by our house if they intended to reach the village, and so the town began to congregate around the man of faith. Most of the other boys, first the younger ones and then the boys my age and older, began to grab tools and sticks and hold them like weapons, and their parents approved of this as if they were doing something noble instead of just being children. Even at my age I knew that no resistance would come from these boys—everyone had to have known—but when it was noticed that I wasn't joining in, that I was not readying to defend the township, I received several concerned looks, and a few villagers even began to point and whisper.

Then the wolves disappeared from view, lost behind the trees as the mountains met the forest, and a hush came over the crowd, the lot of us standing and waiting, hardly breathing.

"Perhaps they are not on their way to the village after all," a nun chimed in, "but instead hunting in the woods, looking for deer," and everyone mumbled hopefully about the validity of what this woman was saying, but then fell silent again as they realized deep down that such a thing was not the case. And yet, the wolves did not emerge. We waited, listening for a warning from the owls, watching the cats watching us, looking for any hint of frightened awareness, but no, nothing. Over an hour had passed since we had lost sight of the wolves, and it was a thirty-minute trip at most on the back of a mount, so gradually, spirits lightened. We were still, the lot of us, horrified, and we stayed waiting for them to emerge, but slowly conversation resumed and people tried to move on from what they had seen. But then, suddenly, there they were, coming from the darkness of the woods, announced with a scream from my little sister who had once again seen them first.

Some of us asked ourselves later why we didn't think to just shoot them, saying that perhaps we could have avoided the whole mess, but seeing the wolves in the light of the sun was almost awe-inspiring, and firing a weapon would have been like shooting at an eclipse, or at a windstorm, or like shooting at a memory. Also, no one had a gun.

"Uncover the eyes of the children," the largest of the three wolves said, his voice quiet, nearly a whisper. He pointed to my mother, her hands shielding my older sister's eyes, and to another woman that I had never seen before that day who was standing with two children hidden beneath her dress. The wolf then pointed to the priest. "If anyone looks away we will burn everything we come in contact with."

"Watch them," the priest told us, trying to force the sound of confidence, his voice shaky and raw.

The large wolf nodded and did his best to smile, and then sat down on a small patch of dried grass while the other two wolves stood over him, glaring down at their brother.

"Begin," the large one said, and the other two lunged forward, ripping through the flesh of the first, pulling off large chunks of meat and then swallowing without hardly chewing at all. We watched the beasts eat the beast, but only because they were watching us, hoping we would look away. When the two wolves had gotten their fill, they left their friend sitting and bleeding, walked back to his mount, pulled out a knife, and slit the bear's throat, then hopped onto their own animals and rode back into the woods, the large wolf falling dead as soon as his brothers were lost in the darkness.

And thus, we were cursed.

a misguided tactic

Blame began to be cast as soon as the wolves had disappeared, our mothers calling out those who didn't worship enough, or sacrifice enough, or who had too many children, or too few—the list of sins was endless. Everyone, it seemed, was to blame except the speaker, but the church, of course, held the most blame of all.

"Explain this," several men demanded, and the priest gave the only explanation he could think of.

"It's the children. Or moreover, a child. A child did this to us."

His reasoning was not well-received, the fathers yelling at him, calling him a charlatan, but still, mothers began to look at their children as if they were parasites, as if we were, all of us, the cause. After a few days, children started to go missing, and nobody would seem to look for them, their parents acting as if everything were normal, as if they had never had children to begin with. The girls seemed to disappear more often than the boys, at least at first, and so in a form of defense the remaining girls began to spread rumors about their brothers and their brothers' friends, how these boys had been acting strange, and speaking nonsense, and lighting fires together, naked in the woods. My friend Matthew was accused of drowning a cat in the pond near town square, while I was said to have taken to wearing women's clothing in the middle of the night, crawling on the ceiling and speaking in words too ancient for man to know. Some boys went missing, but most people saw through the girls' trickery, heard the desperation when they spoke, and decided that they had to be possessed, so, despite their efforts, the girls began to disappear with more frequency.

forked tongue promise

Matthew and I began to catch snakes, the black ones with mouths as white as salt, and then we'd sell them to the neighbors for a few pieces of silver, up to six if the things were still alive. The idea, passed down from the old religion, was that if there was a serpent in your home the evil spirits would assume the devil had already been there and thus move on, ready to lay havoc on another household; prepared to steal someone else's soul.

We knew that the practice was nonsense, Matthew and I both, but if it wasn't us it would be two other boys, and we had our parents to think about.

"Have your folks accused you yet?"

"No," I said as I turned over a rock, chasing a snake the length of my arm. "Not yet. My father is a man of reason."

"And what about your mother?"

"She looks at me a lot, will walk into a room just to look at me. She questions the money I bring home. She tells my father that I'm trying too hard, that I must be hiding something."

He nodded as if he had heard the same thing about himself.

"My sister's gone missing," he said, his face stretched in a way that was hard to read, but it looked like he was smiling. Without warning he lunged forward and caught our snake by the neck, its tail wrapping around his arm, making it look as if it belonged there, like it was an extension of the boy, and then he said, "She's been gone for three days now."

My mouth went dry.

"Elizabeth."

He nodded.

"That was her name, yes."

"Have you said anything to your father?"

"I just asked where she was."

"And what did he say?"

"He said that I was doing a damn fine job with these snakes."

We knew, the both of us, that the snakes would not save a single family that we sold them to, but we knew also that they were saving us, or at the very least, buying us some time.

We didn't leave the forest that night until we each had snakes in both our hands.

whispers of the dead

There was a man who lived on the opposite edge of town from us, a Raleigh, who was said to be able to speak to the dead. He had been called upon more than once to help the town through troubled times, our fathers looking to the wisdom of the ancients to solve the problems of the moment, this man's connection to infinity envied by all men and women of faith.

But he had gone missing the day that the wolves arrived, and stayed missing for months, and then, late one evening, a neighbor had seen candlelight coming from his home, had suspected children of breaking and entering, but upon investigating this neighbor found the man himself, thin, his hair long and wild, mumbling incoherently as he dug through his belongings.

"I was captured," he later told us, "by the wolves. They

held me in the mountains, fed me raw meat, tortured me daily, trying to get me to speak to their ancestors and reveal how best to punish us, to take vengeance against our town for the sins they feel we have committed against nature. But I wouldn't tell them anything, wouldn't help them in any way."

We explained to him what had happened since he had been kidnapped, about the women losing their teeth and hair, about the pregnancies from nowhere, about the priest being burned alive, and though he seem shocked, his eyes wide, he said that he knew these things, that the wolves had spoken of all of it.

"Ask our dead," one of the older men demanded of Raleigh, "what we can do to please the wolves. We worshipped them once, long ago, and we can worship them again if that's what needs to happen."

Raleigh shook his head.

"There is nothing that can be done to appease them. I think it may have been our worship that brought this upon us to begin with."

Raleigh was struck, twice in the mouth, and the old man said it again.

"Ask our dead."

The mystic man was shaken, and it took him several tries before he could channel a spirit, but before long he was embodied by Richard Crawlston, one of the founders of our township and the man who built the church.

"Cut the hair off the children," Richard said through Raleigh, "and bury it at the edge of the woods closest to the mountains. Gather the teeth that have escaped from the mouths of your wives and hang them in pouches, at least three in each one, over the door of every household."

The men waited, and when it was clear that he was finished, Raleigh was struck again.

"That's not enough."

The poor mystic spit a mouthful of blood onto the floor, then looked around the room at the men he knew were craving violence.

"Women who laugh too much," he said, "are diseased, and they should be strangled. Children who argue too much are diseased, and they should be drowned. Burn the beds of the wicked in the center of town. If the smoke goes east, even slightly, then the wolves are pleased. West means there are more sinners yet."

As I looked around the room I saw that most of the men were smiling.

Raleigh had finally said what they wanted to hear.

the love of the father

My father still told me, every day during those tough times, that he loved me. It seemed genuine and not tainted like the love he expressed for Megan, my older sister, his declarations to her changing from a bold statement to a desperate whisper as the nights wore on. But he controlled himself, kept himself locked in his room after dark, much like the morally conscious werewolves of old folklore, the beasts protecting their loved ones from the wrath of their systematic, carnal desires.

"My son," he would say, wrapping his arms around me, "I love you, child," and then he would make promises of how life would get better, and how the townspeople would eventually stop blaming one another for their hardships, telling me that we would find a way to keep on living. "Until then," he said, "you need to make sure not to act in any way peculiar, and to accuse at least one child per week of possession. Choose not only enemies, but friends as well, as your finger-pointing will seem more genuine if it hurts you to say it."

"I remember, father."

And then he would kiss me on the temple and ruffle my hair.

the long-limbed woman

We were still expected to go to school despite the hardships of the village, and every morning, just after the sun came up, we remaining children would walk to our classrooms on the east side of town and begin our studies. It was difficult to watch as our teachers continued to decay, most of them unwed spinsters, drying up, shriveling to nothing, just thin flesh wrapped tightly around brittle bones, but we found that it was even harder to focus on the lessons that we had barely cared about in the first place. What was worse was that our teachers began to crack, falling to pieces as they saw their youth and beauty washed away, their bodies foreign to them, hideous in ways they never could have fathomed, and they began to cast blame for their misfortune, as most of the town did, on the very children they were supposed to help raise into adults. One by one these women would give up on us, or would break and attack her classroom, and so, as teachers fell, the different levels were moved into single rooms, the few dedicated women willing to stick with their profession suddenly burdened with extra students. Children continued to disappear, and so class sizes would shrink a little now and then, the remaining students redistributed, but still we were packed into small rooms, outnumbering the teachers in nearly every case by forty to one.

After Mrs. Henriksen, my teacher from before the town was cursed, stood up one afternoon and grabbed my friend Christopher, by his neck and hair, out from behind his desk and then dragged him to the woods never to be seen again, most of my class, including myself, was moved to Ms. Hubble's room down the hall, normally a fifth year teacher now with students ranging from ages seven to fifteen. She was single, which meant that she still had her hair and teeth, but she was skinny like the rest, made of practically nothing, barely even a human being. Like all of the other women who had lost the urge to eat and sleep, Ms. Hubble's skin was tight on her frame, but thin and dry and wrinkled, always tearing, miniscule amounts of blood trickling down her body, staining her, coloring her like ink on paper. But Ms. Hubble was affected by the curse in a way that had bypassed the other women, our teacher continually getting taller, her limbs growing longer all the time, her chest and head staying roughly the same size they had always been while her legs nearly doubled in length, her arms hanging lower and lower, the woman coming to resemble an insect, and in her mouth she grew extra teeth, long and yellow, like the teeth of an old man. This didn't happen overnight, but you could see the difference from day to day, could see the way her body shifted, and you could imagine the final destination.

Not surprisingly, when Ms. Hubble assigned us homework it always walked in with us the next morning, no excuses, no exceptions.

the harvest

It's hard to think of it now, but the priest was once a beloved man, a source of strength in the community, the one man in town who was involved in the lives of nearly every other citizen. He was chosen as a child from the choir, and then instructed on how to speak to the gods. He wore all black as a representation of our tarnished souls, was the only man allowed the color, and he walked with a cane he didn't need, black as well, to represent the crutch of our sins. He spent most of his time with the children in the choir, and with the sisters of the church, all of them dressed in dark grey, as close as a color could get to black without being black itself.

Among several other things, the priest was in charge of the yearly sacrifices, and of the ritual in which the young women were chosen. Everyone was in the running to die for our sins—all men, women, and children—but the gods always chose a girl, a young lady between the ages of ten and fourteen, or at least that's what the priest announced as the spirits' decision each and every year. I was a finalist once, when I was eight, and I stood there frightened, worried that I would be the first male child in over fifty years to find myself tied to the tree of despair. I was holding hands with my uncle Thomas and a neighbor girl, Bethany—thirteen with brown hair and light freckles, her teeth crooked in a cute way—and she kept crying, bawling her eyes out, while my uncle stood there trying not to smile. We were the last three considered for sacrifice, and it was clear to everyone but me who was going to lose their life.

"Ignore the girl's tears!" the priest said to the town. "Those are not the result of an emotion, but the escape attempts of the spirits that plague her soul! She is the one the gods have selected! She is the one weighed down with evil! Any hardship you have faced this year was the result of this child's sinful heart!"

I held onto her hand as long as I could, even as she was being dragged away, because I had known her, had been her friend, and even though she was a wicked woman I still felt a fondness for her, could hear her silly jokes and old children's songs whispering through my mind, riding on the memory of her voice.

"I'll miss you," I mouthed as I released her hand, but she didn't see me, the crowd already swarming around her, cursing her name for the tragedies that had befallen each family, everything from poor crops to bleeding gums and back again.

the time thief

It was Elizabeth, Matthew's older sister, who was the first confirmed dead of all the children that had gone missing, her body—still mostly intact except for the missing hands —dragged through the streets on a rope tied to her ankles, the girl's mother—bald, toothless, seven months pregnant —pulling her along and yelling at the sky, "She stole my youth and beauty! She stole my life from me! She stole my youth!"

Nobody tried to stop her, and most people didn't even look up as she passed, the whole town acting as if everything that this wretched woman did was perfectly reasonable.

It was only a matter of days before some of the other women began to follow suit, returning to the bodies that they had hidden in the woods and then dragging them through town, showing off their sacrifices to the gods that were clearly ignoring us.

As children we could do nothing but watch.

telltale mice

Dead mice began to show up, by the dozens, in the homes of the elderly. The mice would look fine, not wounded, not bloodied, just a little sunken in, sitting in a way that made it seem as if they had been waiting for death. The old women, all past seventy, most of them bald and toothless before the curse had taken hold and thus rather unaffected by the first few rounds of punishment, had taken to the pregnancies with a certain amount of grace, happy to feel a child in their bodies after decades of being barren. These women even seemed content as they watched their husbands turn from old, broken men into shining examples of vitality, the women showing no bitterness, but rather a sense of admiration for the young-looking bodies that they had long since considered lost to time. But the mice, on the other hand, shook these women, the vermin spread around their homes in what most people would consider to be random placement, but the old women read messages into each corpse found, piecing together their futures from the dead rodents' bodies. Suddenly they began to look at their husbands with frightened contempt.

"You are going to beat me," they would say, or, "You're going to leave me," or, "You're going to murder me in a fit of anger."

The husbands, the old men who looked so young, would argue with their wives, telling these women that they loved them, but the old ladies would persist, yelling these accusations at their husbands, hitting them, throwing a fit every time these men walked into view, until these prophecies came to be, the husbands first leaving and then returning to beat their wives, murdering them in bouts of frustrated rage, one by one until there were no more old women, just old men, lonely and ashamed and waiting for death.

three mothers

There were three of them, standing shoulder to shoulder off in the distance, watching us be children. They didn't look like what we knew of women, mostly because they had full heads of hair and meat on their bones, but they were obviously not just girls, that much was certain. They were dressed in black, a forbidden color for anyone other than the priest, long since dead by then, and their faces were not visible to us, hidden in shadow even though there was no shadow in which to hide them.

"Matthew," I said, "do you see the women? Out towards the trees, dressed all in black?"

"I try not to see anything anymore."

He looked at his shoes as if to prove a point.

I left Matthew and began to walk towards them, these unknown women, but I could never get close, these dark figures always the same distance away from me. I never saw them try and escape, never saw them take even one step backwards, but as I moved they moved, and so I kept pushing them back with my presence until eventually they were past the first line of trees and watching us from the darkness of the woods.

a thousand points of light

One night, when the curse was still fresh, I walked in on my younger sister, Isobel, the one who had first seen the wolves, sitting on the floor with her knees pulled up, crying into her dress. The girl was hardly making a sound—no sniffles, no sobs—having trained herself to cry silently so as not to attract our mother. In the six or so weeks since the wolves had brought the changes in the women, our mother had turned from a neglectful parent into a creature of barbed wire, broken glass, and stone, the woman with nothing but spite and malice running through her veins and a constant look of cold contempt fixed upon her face. Isobel was right to avoid the woman. If it were not for our father I am sure we would have been butchered or abandoned in the woods by the end of the first week.

"What's the matter, Isobel?"

She looked up, surprised, her eyes wide and red. I could see that she was glad it was not our mother, but she was far from pleased to see me in her doorway. Ever since the wolves she had been distant, acting as if she were truly afraid that I was on their side, that I would have stopped her from warning the others if only I had had the chance.

"It's the sky," she said reluctantly. "I miss the sky."

When Isobel was young, hardly able to talk, my father and I would take her out at night and point up to the stars, using our fingertips to trace the constellations that we knew, making up the ones that we had forgotten or had never known, naming them after friends and neighbors, doing our best to make her laugh.

I sighed.

"It's been a while since we've seen it."

She nodded and then turned to her window, her eyes fixed on the clouds that wouldn't move.

"I have an idea," I said stepping into my room for supplies, returning a few moments later with pencils and ink and a small stack of paper. "Let's make a sky in here, one that you can see whenever you want."

For the first time in weeks my sister smiled at me, and then the two of us sat on her floor and drew stars. I went slow with my drawings, not wanting to outdo her, eager for her to feel accomplished about something, but on her insistence I would help her name the constellations, the two of us taking turns back and forth.

"This one's The Grey Fox," she said pointing to a long string of stars.

I smiled.

"And this one is old man Huxley. You can tell from the

hunch in his back."

And with that she burst out laughing, something I had forgotten the sound of, but the joy was short-lived as her amusement had awoken our mother, and before we knew it there she was, standing in the middle of the room, staring at us and not saying a word.

For a long time the woman looked at us, and for a long time we sat in silence.

and my father, he suffered too

Against all reason, my father's teeth unstained themselves, straightened out both top and bottom, and he seemed to grow a half an inch. He began to glow as well, his skin suddenly beautiful, unblemished, and his hands and feet became uncalloused, soft and flawless as if he had never worked a day in his life. My father, like all of the fathers, like nearly every man I knew, had become the perfect specimen of male health, the perfect human.

"I hate what the wolves have done to me," my father said to me one afternoon, the two of us in the kitchen and looking into the living room where my mother, his wife of nineteen years, slept on the couch. "To think that I am so blessed, that I have been given the body of my youth—no, better than that—that I have been gifted the body of a man who has reached his full potential, while your mother has had everything ripped away from her, her youth and beauty replaced with a body that words like 'haggard' and 'repugnant' do not even begin to describe... It just tears me up. To know that your mother wants me more than she ever has, but that I can not even look at her, the woman I love, the woman who has raised my children, without my stomach churning... It is absolutely dreadful."

"Poor old man," my mother said from the couch, her voice thick in the air as if she were standing right in front of us, and behind us, and beside us. "How tough it must be to be beautiful. How awful you must feel to be so repulsed by your own wife. What a tragedy your life has become."

Her eyes stayed closed as she spoke, her body remaining still with only her lips moving, the woman spitting out her words from a toothless mouth.

"Remind me as we fall asleep tonight to pray for you. You shouldn't have to live like this."

And with that my mother started laughing, just a chuckle at first, but soon she had worked her way to a cackle, and then her eyes flew open, she sat straight up, and she stared at her husband and kept laughing and laughing to the point that my father took my hand and led me out of the house, worried for my safety and worried for his own.

That night my father began to sleep on the floor in the living room, or in the hallway outside my sister's door, never once returning to the bed that he had once shared with his wife, though he insisted, to all of us, that he loved her just the same.

the girl with hair
the color of sweet potatoes

As a child in our village you would be pulled aside and asked to choose your favorite god, just you and the priest in a room, a picture of each of the superior beings our ancestors had chosen to worship hung low on the wall, the perfect eye-level for a child of five or six. I could never choose my favorite among them, not drawn to any one specific deity over the rest of them, but time and time again I would be taken into that little office and instructed to select an idol. I would sit with the priest and look at the drawings, hoping my heart would open as he said it would, that I would suddenly feel a strong connection to the mother of the rivers or the man who represented the earth that we walked on and the soil that produced our food, but I felt nothing, and so chose nothing. One day, frustrated, the priest gave me a piece of paper and several colors of ink, then asked me to draw what my soul showed me when I closed my eyes and thought of god. What I drew was a young girl, age thirteen, naked, with copper hair, fair skin, freckles that wrapped around her like the dust on a forgotten sculpture, and a little bit of blood on her legs and torso, not from death but from birth, as if she were born a teenager, escaped from her mother's womb mere moments before.

"This is not god either," I told the priest, "but at least she is real," to which he responded by ripping my drawing to pieces and telling me, in a shaky voice, that my favorite god was the father of the owls, and then he ushered me out, telling me never to speak of what I had drawn.

the eternal unborn

As time went on the pregnant women stayed pregnant, swelling with child, or even children in some cases as it seemed that there were multiple living beings squirming around within the bellies of selected women. Eight, eleven, thirteen months and not a single birth, just growth, and hunger, and back pain. Our mothers became vicious and full of hatred, looking at us remaining children as if we were plagued rats.

"More like you," my mother would say and point to her stomach every time she saw me or my older sister. "More like you."

At night we were forced to put our beds in front of our bedroom doors just to keep her out, afraid of what she might do, the same way my sister Megan was afraid of our father and his pent-up lust.

It was Matthew's mother, a woman already proven to act drastically, that suggested we cut a woman open to see what might come out, trying to convince us that she and all of the other women could potentially be carrying goat babies, or wolves, or some other vile thing. The pregnant women drew straws, and it was the woman I had never seen before the morning of the wolves, the one who had hidden her two children beneath her skirt (the two children, it should be mentioned, that had since gone missing) who proved unlucky. She put up a fight when her straw came up short, as did the beasts within her belly, her stomach rumbling as if its contents were on the edge of boiling, but the town was stronger than she was, and the other women held her down and took a knife to her middle, men standing by with their axes just in case they would have to fight what came out of her. But nothing came out. When the blood stopped spilling and they looked inside her there was nothing—no sons, no daughters, no animals or mythic creatures—just darkness and empty space.

the borrowed girl

Matthew and I began to spend more time together, not so much out of the enjoyment of one another's company—though we were close friends—but simply to avoid being alone. Every day he would come over after school and we would wander off into the woods, walking mostly in silence, staying close to the town, close to my house. We had given up on the snakes, had given up on anything that would make us stand out in the eyes of the villagers, trying instead to fade into the background, to be seen as little as possible.

We were out to exist without existing, and doing a fine job of it.

"I saw my sister," Matthew said one afternoon, his voice a whisper in spite of our seclusion, as if even the trees might lash out at him for admitting something so peculiar.

"When was this?"

"This morning. She was in a house made of mud and straw, tied to a chair, but she was alive, her hands still where they should be."

I sighed a heavy breath.

"Matthew..."

"No, I'm not saying that she's alive, I know she's dead, but I saw a flash of her from before it happened—just a few minutes of her life before my mother brought her back in from the forest..."

He started crying, gently, and I almost touched his arm to comfort him, but then pulled away at the last moment.

"She wasn't dead when my mother walked away that first night. She wasn't..."

He cleared his throat, tried to force himself to stop crying.

"She wasn't cut. Do you remember how fresh Elizabeth's body was when she was dragged through the streets? That's because she only died that morning. I saw it as clear as you're standing here, the vision hitting me like a gust of wind on the way to school today, my sister, Elizabeth, tied to a chair, other children close by, and something else, something just out of reach... Maybe a woman. Maybe several women. And then my mother..."

He stopped and looked off in the direction of his house.

"I could feel my mother coming, walking into the woods, and then the women—I know it now, can almost see it, there were women there—they took a knife and stole my sister's hands."

He sat down and tucked his head between his knees.

"And then they put Elizabeth back where they had found

her, just in time to be reclaimed by the woman who had abandoned her in the first place."

I sat down with him and put my arm around his shoulder, no longer afraid to touch him.

"I don't want you to die," he said, crying again. "I don't want either of us to die. You're all that I have anymore."

He looked at me, obviously hoping that I would say something similar.

"You're my brother," I told him. "You're the only person I'm not afraid of these days."

"We can't come into these woods anymore," he said. "We need to find another way to be invisible. My sister was warning me, and you too. She was warning us from the woods... I see that now."

I in no way believed it, but I promised him that we would protect each other, that neither of us would meet the fate his sister had.

"As long as we have each other," I said, "no one can do us any harm."

the lone wolf

A wolf came down from the mountain, just one by itself, walking on all fours instead of upright, three months to the day from the afternoon those first three came and cursed our town. Isobel, my little sister, like the time before, was the first to notice the wolf as he neared the far side of the forest, and she was hanged immediately after someone pointed out the pattern, my mother and father remaining silent as men and women strung up their daughter, as afraid of her in that moment as they were of the beast that was slowly approaching from the hills.

We waited for what was coming, just as we had the first time.

We could smell the wolf before we saw him, the scent overpowering like the stink of a mass grave, and when the wolf emerged from the woods we saw that he was wounded, alive but rotting as if he were dead. The creature was covered with open sores, maggots and flies and ants crawling all over his body, eating him as he walked along. His eyes were solid white, dead-looking, and his mouth was full of missing teeth with blood and pus dripping from his open jaw. Unlike the wolves that had come before him, he did not stop and demand our attention, but rather walked right past us, slow and steady, continuing on into town. Harold's father stepped forward with an axe but was dragged away by other villagers, all of them afraid of the consequences that would come from killing this now sacred beast.

"We are supposed to honor the wolves," one man whispered.

"We must make atonement," another followed.

Women ran to their homes and grabbed their most valuable pieces of jewelry, their one-of-a-kind family heirlooms, and then returned to the streets and laid them before the wolf, hoping to win his favor, but he just continued to walk, stepping over the offerings, heading diligently towards the middle of town.

And then the crying started, the young woman from before, silent now for weeks, back apparently to honor our guest, sobbing quietly though obviously afraid, her voice coming from the center of the village, from the exact spot where the wolf seemed to be heading. In spite of the circumstances, I found myself aroused in the same way that I had been when she had awoken me from a dead sleep, and I could feel from the shift of energy around me that the other boys and men had been affected in a similar way, their eyes suddenly sharp with determination, their bodies sweating profusely, never mind the cold air. We continued after the wolf, but only because he was walking towards the woman.

In the center of town, just the same as always, there was nothing—no woman, no source of the sound, just the crying surrounding us as if we were in the woman's mouth—and there, right where the woman should have been, was where the wolf stopped, lowered his head and opened his jaw. Out of the wolf came a stream of blood and maggots and worms and flies and spiders and centipedes and rotten flesh and human teeth and clumps of hair—far more than what should have been able to fit inside his body—and then the wolf collapsed and sunk into the mess he made.

And once again, we were cursed.

a gathering in the woods

I began to have dreams soon after our visit from the second wolf, dreams of some of the other children, some my age, some younger, with only one older child making her way in, a Michelle, Jonathan's sister, age sixteen with dark brown hair and hazel eyes. In the dreams I would start off alone, outside of my house, right below my window, looking off into the forest, the night almost pitch black, the clouds blocking the light of the moon and stars. I would begin, with confidence, to walk towards the darkness between the trees, and then I would be joined by the others—first Lillian, then Moses, then Jeremiah, then Madeline, until there were nine of us, Michelle being the last one to join the procession. In the woods we would sit in a circle and begin to speak, but the words were too low for me to decipher, our speech half-whispered, but whatever it was that we were saying it was powerful, and a fire would start in the circle we had formed, small but bright, with no smoke produced by the flame.

In the light of the fire I would notice that Matthew was not among us, and then my eyes would flutter open and the dream would be over.

the murder

There was a murder, when I was a child, maybe seven or eight, that went unpunished, that no one seemed to want to solve. It was a young couple that was killed, both of them born and raised in our town, their ancestors among the first settlers, the young woman a direct descendent of Richard Crawlston, the man who had led the expedition into the forest and founded our church.

The wedding, I remember, was attended by nearly half the town, and everyone, it seemed, wished them well. He was a blacksmith, had done the work for years, first with his father and then he went out on his own, focusing his efforts on tools and utensils, while the old man worked on weaponry and armor, the men's shops set up next door to one another, sharing a common wall. The young man was blonde like his father, and taller than most men, with a square jaw and a slightly crooked nose, broken in his rowdy youth. His wife, the Crawlston by birth, was beautiful, and from what I remember, funny, always laughing and playing tricks on us children, stealing our noses and making small objects disappear and reappear on command. She looked like her mother, small in frame, dark hair, with big eyes, thin lips, and a toothy, infectious smile.

She got pregnant right away, and the town swelled with pride as if every man and woman we knew had had a hand in it. The anticipation of the child was the only topic of discussion for at least a month leading up to the birth, everyone eager to see the offspring of two such physically attractive people, all of us speculating on whose features the child would have and whether or not they would produce a son as their first born, a sign of good luck not only for them but for the town. Finally, late one autumn evening, our questions were answered when the young mother went into labor and the child was brought into the world. I was there with my mother, waiting outside with other eager families, longing to get a look at the child who had dominated our thoughts and prayers for so many months, but when the priest and his nuns walked out of the house they looked winded, as if they had been punched in the stomach, not once but over and over and over again. The priest would not speak to us, just walked back home to hide in the church, and so we rushed, against the wishes of the new father, into the home to see what had happened.

I expected, as I'm sure many others did as well, to see a stillborn son, a dead child as hard as a stone held in the arms of a crying mother, but instead we saw the woman holding a healthy looking little girl, the child with fair skin and a decent amount of hair, all of it as red as the earth's clay, which was something I had never seen before. The couple looked at our mothers, and our mothers looked back at the new parents.

"She is just a girl," the young man pleaded. "She is just our daughter, and on her head is only hair. It doesn't mean anything. She is not what you think she is. We know we can't stay here, and we don't plan to. We will leave as soon as my wife is fit for travel, three days at most. Give us three days. We are in love, not just with each other, but with our daughter. Give us three days and you will never see us again."

Our father made my sisters and me stay home the next day, worried of how it all might affect us, but Joshua, an older boy, had seen the house, had told us protected few what had happened to the new family.

"There was blood," he said, "everywhere, and pieces of them, small chunks, barely recognizable, all over the place. They didn't look like people anymore, their skin stretched, not cut but ripped, as if they had been pulled apart, torn like paper. And the child, the poor little girl, was fixed to the wall, so many nails in her that it was hard to tell what you were looking at, and they had removed her scalp, the hair that I heard described as the color of flame missing from the scene, taken by one of the men who did this."

"They?" an older girl scoffed. "One of the men? What do you mean?"

"There were at least three of them, probably several more. There is no way that one man could have done all of this alone."

"Why didn't they burn the house?" another girl said.

"I think," he continued, lowering his voice, slightly afraid himself of what he was about to say, "that they are proud of what they've done."

The home was eventually burned, later on the next afternoon, by Raleigh and my father and several other men of moral strength, all of them eager to rid our town of such an awful place, desperate to destroy the home of the most grizzly crime our town had seen in at least a decade.

Despite mentioning them almost every day for half a year, none of our parents spoke of the couple, or the girl with the autumn red hair, or their quaint little home, ever again.

.

the man who spoke to the dead

There had been concern expressed about Raleigh's safety, townspeople afraid that he might be stolen again by the wolves and used as a tool against us, and so he was appointed guardians—three strapping young men armed with axes, hired to stay with Raleigh at all times, sleeping in shifts, keeping him constant company. It was clear to anyone who wanted to see it that we were his captors, that he had not been kidnapped but had run away from the village, that we were the ones he was afraid of, but most of us wanted to believe that he was on our side; that he could save us; that his connection to the dead would be the key to our salvation.

"There are sinners yet," he said, exhausted, always tired,

worn ragged by his ever-present companions. Raleigh, unlike the other men in the village, had never begun to look young—never lost the grey in his hair, never had his skin pull tight and shine like the flesh of the youth, never lost the yellowness in his eyes that comes from years of drink—but rather seemed ravaged by age, the stress of his new life taking a constant toll on his body. "As long as there are wretched souls there will be punishment. There is no escaping that."

"Who are these sinners?" a man asked, thumbing the blade of a knife, eyeing his wife and child, obviously hoping that they would be named.

"The spirits do not tell me these things," he said, then paused, almost reluctant to say the next part. "For my own safety, I believe, the dead withhold this information. If I started naming names the wicked would feel threatened, would come for me. I can't say anything because I don't know anything. As soon as I do, I will be dead."

"Maybe you'll be dead anyway," the man with the knife said in a tone as sharp as his blade.

"Maybe I will, but when I go the dead will go with me. Unless another oracle comes forward, I am all you have."

Of course the man was beaten for saying such things, with even his guardians throwing a few punches his way, but the men kept it light, aware that what the old man said was true. My father never hit Raleigh, even helped him to his feet after most of the others had left, and though he thanked my father the man looked at me when he spoke, our eyes locked, a genuine smile on his face. "Thank you. May a thousand blessings fall to you."

And then my father grabbed me by the hand and led me home.

homecoming

One evening, just before sunset, four months after the wolves had first come to visit, one of the missing children found her way back into town, Eloise, an eleven year old girl with short dark hair and a slight underbite. We were shocked—not so much that she returned, but that she was the first. Forty or so children had disappeared by that point, and none of them had come back into town, and then, out of the blue, a girl returned after having been absent for nearly twenty days.

Some of us boys were standing around, done with schoolwork and chores but afraid to have fun, afraid of the negative attention our laughter might bring, when we saw her walking in from the northern woods, coming from the direction of the lake. Her skin had a blue hue to it—we could tell even from a distance—as if she were freezing, or perhaps a walking corpse, blue and bloated after a month of being tied to something heavy deep below the surface of the water. Stephen, a younger boy, thought she was a ghost and ran home to hide in the arms of his parents, but the rest of us stayed, silently waiting, taking note of her staggered steps, the way that her left foot was slightly dragging. She tried to call out to us, but the sounds she formed were not quite words.

We went to her anyway.

"Eloise," I said, "where have you been?"

She mumbled, but we couldn't understand her. She was in bad shape. We expected her to be skinny, but she had actually gained a little weight, fat mostly, her muscles withering away from lack of use. She had wounds all across her body, bite marks, almost playful, spread across her neck and chest like the affection from an aggressive lover's mouth, but when we looked closer we could see evidence of two rows of teeth, the mouth of the biter hardly anything human, and there were small holes on her limbs as if she had been stabbed with a pencil, or punctured with a large nail. Nothing seemed to be healing, everything open as if fresh, but dark and smelly as if the flesh itself was dead.

"There are three of them," she finally said, "women without faces... Perhaps the faces are there, but they are always hidden... They have mouths... They have proven to me, time and time again, that they have mouths, but when you look at them there is no face to speak of... They hardly speak themselves, but when they do it is as if the walls are speaking... Their whispers, always whispers, come to you from everywhere at once, as if the air were talking, as if these three were everything, as if they spoke for the earth itself..."

From off in the distance Stephen's parents began to approach, and when his mother saw who we were talking to she ran off in the direction of Eloise's parents' house, but her husband started to holler at us, telling us to leave the girl alone, quickening his pace, hoping to scare us off. We kept her talking, knowing that once the adults arrived she would be silenced, taken away from us, lost to us forever.

"Did you see any of the others?"

Something like regret took hold of her face.

"No, but I could hear them... The three women, they eat them... They eat us... They eat everything but the hands... They keep the hands... They say they need them..."

"How did you get away."

"I think they let me go..."

"Did they find you in the forest, or were you handed over?"

"I wa..."

Stephen's father pushed me away from the girl, yelling his head off, "I told you boys to go home! Didn't you hear me?"

"Please!" She burst into tears, a sudden strength pulsing through her veins. "Please hide me! Lock me up! I need a bath, and new clothes, and I need to be locked away! Please don't let them have me again!"

"Shhh," the man said, rocking Eloise in his arms. "Your mom and dad are on their way."

At the mention of her mother, Eloise shrieked and began to kick and thrash, trying to get away from this man's arms, but he held tight until she bit him, his surprise giving her the moment she needed to break free. Eloise made it a few steps, but before she could get far he jumped up behind her and grabbed her by the hair, then held her down and waited for her parents, cooing in her ear, telling her that everything would be just fine.

She was missing again by the next morning, and so was Stephen, and Samantha, and two other little girls.

in a house made of hair

I had a dream once, long before the wolves came down the mountain, about Raleigh, the man who could speak to the spirits. We were in a house made of hair, with millions of golden brown and copper strands woven together to make the walls and floor and ceiling, and he was standing in the corner, much larger than he was in waking hours, whittling something from a block of wood, speaking to me in a warm, fatherly tone.

"There are things," he said, "that only children see, sounds that only children hear, changes in the air that only children feel, and so, when the time comes to act, it is only the children who can respond, only the children who can do the things that need to be done."

Raleigh set down his block and knife and then began, slowly, to walk towards me.

"There are things that only I can see, like the dead standing here with us in this room, dressed in blood and gore the way that you and I wear fur and cotton, begging for revenge against those who have brought them harm, who have cursed them to an eternity of grief and solitude."

He reached out to me and stroked my face.

"And there are things that only you can see—what they are, I do not know, nor can I say their relevance, but it will come to you, and when it does you can not be afraid of it."

And then the hair unraveled, pulling itself apart and receding into the earth, and Raleigh and I were left standing in the darkness of the forest, surrounded by the watchful eyes of beasts we could not see, creatures hidden in the shadows of the woods.

"This is your home, child. The world is your home. Your bones are your home. No one can ever take your home away from you, or you away from it. Remember that."

And then everything went black.

long in the tooth

At first glance the classroom was empty, but as we walked in we saw Ms. Hubble perched in the corner, halfway up the wall, sobbing, covering her face with one hand, keeping her balance with the other. We stood near the entrance, too frightened to sit but nearly just as fearful of what might happen if we were to try and leave, and then Ms. Hubble, suddenly aware of us, uncovered her face and tried to speak, but all that came out was a garbled mess. I thought it was her sorrow getting in the way of speech, but then I realized it was her teeth—too many, too big—ruining her mouth for conversation. She had, all of a sudden, just days before, begun to grow again, and now it seemed that she was changing in other ways—weird protrusions coming in under her dress, slits like future eyes forming on her forehead and cheeks, thick, coarse, dark hair coming in on her arms and neck, her skin turning grey, becoming slightly shiny, and the teeth, so many extra teeth... She was crying, of course, in part for herself, but also for us. As horrific as she had physically become, Ms. Hubble was the only one among the few remaining educated women who seemed to hold no ill will towards us children, the only teacher left who seemed to still care about her position and her duty to train us and guide us into adulthood, as bleak as our futures were sure to be.

She took chalk and wrote on the board, and in a surprisingly clean script considering her condition.

I'M SORRY. THERE'S NOTHING ELSE I CAN DO
FOR YOU. GET OUT. STAY OUT. NEVER COME
BACK HERE.

She stayed behind when we left, blacking out the windows with newspaper and scrap, pushing her desk in front of the door to keep us—and everyone else—out of her classroom. Half of us went to Ms. Cooper, most of the rest went to Mrs. Rockwell, and three or four of us went missing.

a man among men

In our village I was treated—not by the women but by a good number of the men—as an adult from the age of eleven, three years before the wolves' arrival. My father had fallen ill early that autumn, taken by a great pox that had left him fevered and swollen, unable to eat and hardly able to breathe, and it seemed very likely that he would die. He called me to his bed, close enough to speak but still far enough that I might not be struck by his illness, giving me instructions on how to tend the crops. I had spent a little time out there throughout the spring and summer, but not enough to feel confident in taking on the fields alone, but my father assured me that any man who would lend his help, even Carlton, Matthew's father, my father's closest friend, would only do so to try and take claim on part of our yield, and so I was to do all of the work myself if I wanted our family to survive the winter. During the early hours of the day and all the way through the peak of the afternoon I would tend our crops, preparing for harvest, and then, as it got close to sundown, I would return home to study my lessons on the insistence of my father, nearly dead but still holding on, guiding our family as best as he could from the bed my mother had made for him in the shed just outside of our house.

In my mind it was my sister, Megan, the older of the two girls, then age thirteen, that sacrificed the most, tending to my father when my mother had written him off as dead, feeding him broth when he was able to eat, reading stories to him in the evenings after she had finished with her chores, and it was because of her efforts that he got through the spell and was well again, back on his feet just in time to help me with harvest.

After that my father insisted to the men of our village that I be considered one of them, that I, like every other man who takes care of a family, should have every right to attend town meetings and to be present any time important matters were discussed, issues that may in fact impact the family that I was sworn to protect. Not every man felt that this was valid, but a majority did, and so it was honored and I became a man in their eyes.

I still, however, had to go to school, as unnecessary as it seemed to be, and I was still unable to drink, and I still had a curfew, but damn it all, I was a man.

gifts of the spirit

What were once considered gifts in our church had become the mark of evil in our streets, and those known to speak in tongues, or to heal the wounded, or to discern the nature of unknown men were fingered, dragged into the streets and killed for failing to protect us from the darkness that ravaged every aspect of our daily lives. Raleigh, of course, was spared, seen as an asset by too many townspeople for anyone to murder him on a whim, his life protected by the same thing that kept him captive, but the rest of them were not so lucky, these people systematically murdered as the curse progressed, the masses convinced that their blood would make a difference.

The murder that stands out the most is that of Loretta Peterson, a school teacher for the young, first year, I believe—a friendly but perhaps overly-mindful young woman who stayed unmarried despite her good looks and several offers, abstaining because she had never fallen in love, something a bit unheard of in those days. She had been a big part of the church from the age of ten or so, the youngest woman in our town to ever be blessed with the gift of tongues, speaking what sounded like nonsense to me but like the words of our gods to so many others, moving these fellow church-goers to tears, dropping them to their knees, overwhelming them with faith. Once the crown jewel of our congregation, Loretta became an agent of dark spirits in the eyes of the people once the curse took hold, and thus needed to be put to death, burned in the center of town as punishment for calling the wolves down from the hills with her ancient, forgotten language. The crowd pulled her out of her house late one afternoon, a gag in her mouth to muffle the screaming, then stripped her bare and tied her to a stake with thin metal wire, all the while yelling insults, spitting on her, hitting her with whatever they could get their hands on. As they prepared the logs beneath her feet for the flames that would devour the woman, Carlton, Matthew's father, a frequent participant in these killings, removed the gag and asked her what she had to say for herself, what excuse she might provide for betraying her brothers and sisters to the spawn of the devil.

"I never spoke in tongues!" she shouted through her tears. "I never said anything! I made it all up! I was a little girl when I started, and I did it as a joke, to make my friends laugh, but then everyone else believed in it so I had to keep going! I did it for you! I did it to keep your faith alive! To make you feel safe! I did it for my parents! I did it for the children!"

Her confession moved me, but her ploy did not work, instead the crowd just hit her harder, yelling about how it must have been her dishonesty, her mockery of the spiritual gift that had angered the gods and brought the wolves' wrath upon us.

As a town, with the sun just starting to set in the west, the people lit the girl aflame.

matthew

Matthew went missing. His sister had been dead for months and months, her murder so out in the open that by lasting as long as he did we had all considered him to be safe, protected somehow from his mother's wrath; from her ever-accusing finger; from the blame that she just couldn't stop spouting. It had taken the other children several days before they realized that the boy was missing, but I had known about his disappearance from day one, had known every little detail of what had happened to him, because I saw it in a dream the night it transpired, possibly in real time.

In the dream I saw Matthew lying in bed, trying to sleep but restless, afraid of his mother once again after months of indifference, worried about her sudden sweetness, her insistence that he help himself to seconds at dinner, about the way that she kept asking him questions regarding his day, and his schoolwork, and his spirits in general, touching him every chance she got with gentle, but jittery hands. That night when she walked into his room he could not hear her but felt her presence, and though he had wanted to turn and fight her he stayed still, hoping she would lose her nerve and walk away. There was a blow to his head, from what he did not know, but I knew it to be a brick taken from the fireplace. He was dazed by the attack but still conscious, and so he was hit again, the swing knocking him out, and then struck twice just to do it, the satisfaction from the violence overwhelming to his assailant.

Matthew woke up some twenty minutes later, being dragged by one leg into the forest, not, as he had expected, by his mother, but by his father, an elderly man, almost twice his mother's age, who now looked twenty-five thanks to the wolves and their dark ritual. Matthew didn't want to, but he noticed the blood sprayed up the sleeve of his father's shirt and realized that it was this man who had struck him in his bed, that his mother may have willed this into motion, but it was his father who was setting out to murder him, just as, the boy realized, he had likely murdered Elizabeth. He spoke to his father, called out to him, even addressed him by his first name, but the man never looked down, determined to go through with this vicious deed, convinced that there was no other way. Matthew became desperate, called out to the wolves for mercy, asked them to forgive his father and his mother both, and to forgive the entire township for whatever sins they may have committed to bring the beasts' wrath upon us, but Matthew's requests came back unanswered, as the wolves had nothing to do with this violent act, had no desire for men to abandon their children, to beat them and strangle them and leave them in the woods, but the ones responsible heard every word, the three of them standing in the shadows, shoulder to shoulder, their faces hidden as they always were, and when the father finally let the boy go and returned to the village the three women swept in and surrounded the child, repeating his prayers back to him in a unified whisper, laughing at his foolish pandering, dragging him back to their cabin to feed the boy and keep him alive as long as their whim allowed.

an ever-shrinking room

My sister, Megan, the older one, the surviving one, began to make a dress from the sheet on her bed, not, it seemed, because she needed new clothing, but just to give herself something to do. The house had grown stale and quiet after Isobel had been taken from us, with even my father reduced to silence most days. We just had nothing to say to each other anymore, so we all took up our own hobbies. My sister, as I mentioned, would sew; I would play with paper, folding it to make boats and kites; my father returned to the fields to work the soil, though it was clear the ground was poisoned and that nothing would grow; and my mother just looked at her wedding photo, the only picture that she had ever taken with my father, mumbling about how beautiful the man had become since the wolves had paid a visit.

We found comfort in distraction, or discomfort in

obsession, but all of us were busy.

"What are you making today?" my sister asked one afternoon, leaning against my door frame with the dress in her hand. "Another kite?"

"Another kite," I said.

"You think you might fly this one?"

I laughed, not because she had said anything funny, but because we both knew how foolish it was to even consider doing something so joyful in the public eye.

"I doubt it, but I would love to."

She looked at me for a few moments, though clearly her mind was elsewhere.

"Well, I'll leave you to it."

"No," I said, "please, come sit with me."

Megan walked into to my room and sat down beside me, so close that her long hair—worn down, it seemed, out of spite for our mother—brushed lightly against my arm with every movement. We worked in silence, her on her dress, me on my kite.

I couldn't help but focus on my sister as we sat together. The two of us had been born two years apart, down to the week, so despite being a bit younger than her it often felt as if we were twins. Not that we got along, because we rarely did, but when we had our moments it felt so natural, as if we needed one another just to be ourselves. Additionally, we looked like each other, a perfect mix between our mother and father, where Isobel had resembled only our dad, her eyes further apart than ours, her lips thinner, her ears large and low on her head.

"The dress is for Isobel," Megan said, reacting to me as if she could hear my thoughts about our sister and her distinctive features. "I can't seem to make anything for myself anymore... Even though she'll never use them, I've been making her clothes for weeks."

I nodded.

"I named a boat after her," I said.

"She hated the water. You should give her a kite instead."

"I will. I'll give her this one."

She smiled at me, and then let it fade as her mind moved elsewhere.

"Do you remember," she said, "when we were little, that there was The Great Rain? It fell steady for three weeks, just constant water, day in and day out, the wind blowing sheets of it against our house, breaking the window in Isobel's room and nearly pulling off the roof... I was seven then, so you must have been five."

I nodded.

"I do. I remember all of that."

"Well there was an afternoon where Sebastian... Do you remember him?"

She was talking about an older boy who had watched after us now and then when we were young, the boy a woodsman from an early age who set out on his own when the girl he loved became pregnant with another young man's child, making Sebastian one of very few people I had ever known to leave the town.

"Of course I remember Sebastian."

"Well one afternoon he took you and me for a walk, maybe three or four days after the rain had stopped, and we found a puddle—maybe half a foot deep, no more than three feet wide—with a trout in it, just stuck swimming in place. We couldn't figure out how he had gotten there, because we were so far from the creek with no other water around, but there he was. I suggested the wind, but Sebastian didn't know. Anyway, I wanted to carry the fish to running water, to save him from what was sure to come, but Sebastian said it was too far of a walk and that the fish would likely die of shock along the way. He gave us two choices. We could either kill it right then, putting the fish out of its misery with a rock or against a tree, or we could leave it to wait out the shrinking pool, letting it die on its own."

"As to feed another animal," I said.

"Right," she said, "to feed another animal."

"And we walked away."

"Exactly. We left it to die alone in an ever-shrinking existence, the world literally closing in and suffocating it. That's what we felt was the best thing to do."

I could see it on her face that she wanted to compare herself to the fish, but I knew that she would never say such a thing out loud.

"Maybe," she said, "we should have let him kill the fish."

"Perhaps, but I think we should have just gone and fetched a bucket."

She laughed and said, "Of course, a bucket. I've walked around with that for years, and all we had to do was get a bucket."

"But we were children then, Megan."

"We're still children now, love. All this time has passed and all we are is children."

When I finished the kite a few minutes later, I wrote Isobel's name on the front and gave it to Megan, asking her to hold onto it until our sister came back to claim it. When she finished the dress the next morning she gave it to me, asking me to do the same.

the glorious alternative

It was such a natural thing to happen that we couldn't believe it had taken so long—over a year from when the wolves first came in—but then there she was, Geoffrey's mother, a once young and beautiful woman transformed into a monster like the rest of them, her body swinging from a tree near the schoolhouse, the first of the women to commit suicide.

It was the afternoon that they drew straws to see who would be cut open—the day our mothers discovered that there was no end in sight to their so-called pregnancies— that Helen Jorgenson, Geoffrey's mother, walked home from the congregation, grabbed a length of rope, headed to one of the biggest trees in the village, a tree her son and I had climbed together a hundred times or more, and then did the work to stop her breath.

No one was all that upset from the death, but rather somewhat relieved that it had finally come to pass; that someone had ended their own plight; that someone had taken control of their own grisly situation. Suicide washed over the town, with one out of every eight adults ending their lives within the first week after Helen tied the noose around her neck, several of these men and women taking a family member or two with them, the people dying eagerly, as if they had just been waiting for permission.

All of a sudden, thanks to the pioneering of one cowardly woman, there was a new way to die in our quaint little town.

the tragic death
of jennifer bromely

In the death of Jennifer Bromely, I alone am to blame, and it haunts me every waking moment, the girl's face still fresh in my mind, as familiar as the sunrise, or the smell of peach blossoms in the early summer months.

Jennifer was twelve, and the only sister of Eugene, an older boy we all looked up to as being funny, charismatic, kind to everyone no matter what their age, and very protective of his little sister, taking the girl with him wherever he would go, including her in every aspect of his daily life. It was my fondness for him which led to the girl's death, my convincing him to play ball with me and several of the other children, aligning myself with him, making sure that I ended up on his team, which meant that I would be playing against Jennifer. Though close, the siblings were playfully competitive against one another, purposefully never being on the same team during games just to keep things interesting, and, perhaps, to avoid accusations of favoritism.

The game started off well enough, the sky cloudy as always but the weather warm, no problems from any of our mothers, no work to do in the fields, all of us left alone to be children, happy to be involved in a game and not stuck inside watching our families fall to pieces. My team was losing by six points by the time we made it to the third round, even with Eugene on our side, and as we took the field all of us gave each other stern looks, resolved to turn the game around, letting each other know that this was serious, that the time for tomfoolery was behind us. It was Jennifer's turn to kick as the teams traded spots, the lanky young girl who was too thin to be attractive but still charming and funny and a hell of an athlete, stepping up to kick, ready to run, determined to move those skinny legs and get the point; determined to put my team even further behind.

Everything seemed to happen in a moment's time, just a flash and there we were, Jennifer bloody on the ground, being dragged to her death, but I know it happened slowly, can remember every detail when I sit down and try to conjure the memory. The pitch—rolled by her brother—had a spin to it, and Jennifer's kick, strong but misguided, sent the ball up in the air, towards me but falling short, so I ran forward and caught it after the bounce. She was running swiftly, the point still hers if she wanted it bad enough, and with no one close enough to tag her out I was forced to give chase. I ran as hard as I ever had, uninterested in letting my team down, my legs on fire from the strain, and like a sign of approval from the heavens the clouds broke behind me and for the first time in months the sun shined down, casting my shadow forward between Jennifer and I, my silhouette brushing her feet, leading my eyes down, causing me to accidentally bring about her death. I stopped dead in my tracks, dropped the ball, and, with all my strength, fought the urge to cover my mouth and yelp. Jennifer tagged base and my team groaned, yelled at me for letting her get away, but I just stood there, trying to pull myself together. Eugene approached me and patted my back just as the clouds closed up and hid the sun, the boy letting me know that it was all right, that there was still plenty of game left to play, but he stopped when he saw my face.

"What is it?"

"Try not to react," I said, "because I've already attracted too much attention, but your sister, Jennifer... She has no shadow."

"What are you saying?"

"When the sun broke through I could see it wasn't there... The clouds, they must diffuse the light, making it hard to notice, but she has no shadow. She should, but she doesn't. There is nothing there."

"Jennifer," he called out, trying to keep his calm. "Come out here please."

"Don't make trouble," I told him, "I'm sure she's fine. We just need to find someone else without a shadow, someone they won't kill, someone with a voice in this town, and point them out first..."

She approached, smiling awkwardly, confused but not worried.

"Don't tell her," I whispered. "You'll only scare her."

"Stand still," he told her, then looked at her feet, at mine, at his own. With the clouds in the way we barely had shadows at all, but you could see, if you looked hard enough, that ours were there, his and mine, and that hers clearly was not.

"What is it?" she asked, the smile fading from her face, but before I could say anything to comfort her Eugene smashed his fists against her mouth, first one and then the other, over and over until she fell, and then he took his feet to her chest, to her mouth, and to her throat, yelling as he destroyed the young girl, yelling out to the other children, yelling out to the world at large.

"Witch! She is a witch! She has no shadow! She is a demon! She is a witch!"

He reached down and grabbed his little sister by the hair and began to drag her to the center of town, screeching about the devil, yelling at the other kids to go and get some adults, to come back with wood, and nails, and flame, to help him cast this demon, this girl he once loved, "Back to Hell where she belongs!"

I went home rather than staying to watch, passing my mother and remaining sister along the way, both of them eager to see the young witch put to death.

the divorce

We woke to the sound of women's voices, a steady shrieking coming from down the road, with one voice rising above the others; steady—determined; passionately angry. My sister Megan and I dressed and started towards the ruckus, frightened to see almost thirty women congregated—our mother among them—chanting and jumping, touching one another, while Matthew's mother stood on the roof of her home, her hands cupped around her mouth, the obvious source of the movement.

"...while our children stand by doing nothing, giving us no love or comfort, sucking the life from us like spiders drain their prey, and just like those creatures our children should be vanquished! Cast out of our homes! Flattened beneath our weight!"

The women cheered below and Matthew's mother stood

still for a moment, basking in the glory.

We found our father, watching from a distance as many husbands were, and we joined him, both of us grabbing on to one of his hands, our eyes drifting, just as his were, from the woman on the roof down to our mother yelling along with the crowd, and then back to their leader as she began again with her sermon.

"You do not sleep with a serpent, you do not invite the devil into your home for supper, but you allow these beasts, day in and day out, to drain you of every emotion, of every moment of joy, just so they can grow and replace you? You gave them life, and now as you suffer, this wretched curse causing your body to attack your soul and mind, they do not comfort you! No, they reject you! They call you hideous! And vile! And they cower from you in fear! I say give them something to be afraid of! Rise against your children as they would rise against you! And your husbands—when was the last time you felt the loving hand of your husband? When did he last caress your cheek or run his fingers down the small of your back? When did you last hear him whisper into your ear, telling you..."

"You are a witch!" her husband yelled, climbing up the side of the house, a hatchet in one hand, a knife in the other. "Do not listen to this creature," he said to the women below, "She is a sinner! A monster! A plague on this town! And it has nothing to do with how she looks!"

She kept talking, trying to keep the women riled, but he spoke louder, full of fire and self-imposed righteousness.

"This woman had me kill our children! My Matthew and Elizabeth, savagely beaten and then cast out into the forest to wait for death, because she convinced me that it would return her body to her! That it was their lives, not her sins, that turned her into this dreadful beast! Her vanity slew my children, and now she wants you to do the same? You are cheering on a murderer, ready to turn on your own husbands, and why? Because she wants company in hell?"

"He murdered our children!" she said. "You heard it from his own mouth! I told him to take them away, that they were draining me, draining the both of us, and he took it upon himself to murder them! Because he wanted to! This man is th..."

She coughed up her last words as the knife slid in below her ribs, and then it was pulled, with a great fury, down and back, her large stomach splitting open, a thick black liquid spilling forth, the same substance escaping through her mouth and throat, coming up in rhythmic pulses. What was nothing but space in one pregnant woman was now black sludge in another, and we suddenly realized that it was possible that each woman carried something different, that the curse was likely tailored to fit the personality of each woman it affected.

As the crowd began to disperse, our father let go of our hands, called out to his wife, and then walked the shaken woman home, his arm around her shoulders, his head leaning towards her own.

the hayman

There was a man, when I was a child, that would stalk the forest late at night, his face hidden beneath a burlap sack, his clothes stolen from a farmer's scarecrow, and thus he was called The Hayman. The Hayman was a killer of cats, a collector of pieces, a man that would chase and corner and butcher felines, the night of his attacks seemingly random, sometimes coming only once a month, other times two nights in a row, skip a night and then back for three. He was often seen, and often chased, but he was fast, and for nearly a year his identity stayed hidden.

All through his campaign we feared for our lives. We, as a town, had worshipped the cats, had looked to them for safety and strength of spirit, and here was this man, one of our own, who had taken it upon himself to slaughter these animals, leaving pieces of them on the doorsteps of family homes, keeping most of the animal for himself, a souvenir of his viciousness, of his moment of pure control. Eventually I began to question our faith, for though he desecrated our most beloved creature, time and time again, against every belief we held comeuppance never came, no great retribution, the town unpunished for the man's vile sins.

This man was eventually caught, turned in by his son, and as punishment for his deeds, the man, along with his wife and all three of his children, including the one who had handed him over, were taken to the forest and nailed, upside down, to red spruce trees, none of the family facing one another, so that each of them would die alone.

When I was still young but a bit older, the winter after The Hayman was caught, owls began to die because of a parasitic bug. I can't remember what it was exactly, but there it was, a little fly, or flea, or mite dropping these birds in record number, birds that we worshipped for their perception and strength against the elements, taken down, in the hundreds, by a miniscule, bloodsucking parasite— hardly the death befitting a sacred creature, proving in my mind that they were birds and nothing more.

And yet, we worshipped.

like anchors in the earth

In the faith of our fathers there are demons who exist as weights, abominations that are born into existence to tether themselves to sinners, to punish men and women through the generations, the curse handed down the same as one's height or the color of a person's eyes. There are many transgressions that will bring these demons into being, such as familial killings, or the act of bestiality, or theft from one's parents, but the most common sins would be those of adultery, or incest, or if a man and a man should lie together. Until the wolves came, these stories were considered just that—stories, fables, warnings away from activities that would "harm" the commonwealth—but after the curse the people began to imagine themselves weighed down by their sins, by the sins of their parents, or, as was more often the case, these people would see their friends and neighbors as wretched souls, would see them dragging dozens of demons around with them, a combination of bad blood and bad deeds slowing their lives down to a crawl.

In the stories, from the breath of our grandfathers and from the scripture itself, it is said to be possible, if a heart is dark enough, to bring the demons from their realm of existence into our own, to actually see these beasts and their tethers to one's body, allowing them the opportunity to physically harm the sinner that they plague rather than just the ability to hound their souls and control their luck. These demons—different creatures for different sins, some of them women with black eyes who give birth to serpents, some of them men with the faces of rodents and mouths where their hands should be—are said to devour the sinner who calls them into our world and then take their place in society, to wear their skin, communing with the other villagers, using this new disguise to convince others into committing sins that might bring about more demons.

Now whether the townspeople actually believed these things or were just using the concepts as an excuse to murder their wives, their neighbors, and their children is hard to say—all I know for certain is that there were a lot of men in our village who began to speak of these demons on a regular basis, and that the longer a person stayed out of the conversation the more likely they were to be accused of being one of the demons themselves.

In the faith of our fathers.

In the faith of our fathers.

the tragic death of eugene bromely

After the death of Jennifer Bromely, I became a topic of discussion.

The girl's brother, my friend Eugene, had told the town that I had suggested hiding the reality of his sister's missing shadow, that I had said that we should wait and find someone else, someone who "they" would not kill, and so, the question was asked, everyone wondering just who I thought "they" were.

"The wolves," I said, my father standing bravely beside me, the possibility that he could be murdered for his support if they should find me guilty not lost on either of us.

"What exactly did you mean by what you said?"

"I didn't mean anything. I was in shock. I didn't know what to say. I was afraid that Eugene was going to attack me for pointing out the wickedness of his sister, as I expected that he too might be tarnished, seeing as he had always been so fond of the girl, kissing her and taking her with him wherever he went, the two of them often sneaking off together, avoiding the rest of us for hours on end."

I realized what I was saying, and I could feel my father's anxiousness, the man glad that my survival instincts were intact but burdened by the sound of his son speaking false accusations to save his own neck. Eugene may not have been incestuous with his sister, but he had actively participated, very heavily, in her murder, and in my mind he was the perfect scrap to throw to the dogs, especially in the place of myself.

"He's lying," Eugene muttered, seemingly unsure of himself.

He should have known better than to call an accuser a liar, should have known that in our town saying such a thing was the same as a confession, that the only way to combat words said against you was to embrace them, explain them in another context, and move the sin to someone else. And, of course, it helps to act naive.

"Lying about what?" I said. "I was afraid of you, Eugene, afraid that you would protect the sister you had spent so much time with and attack me in her place."

"He's right," another boy said, "Eugene was always sneaking off with her, the two coming back with their clothes all askew, smelling of sin."

"And they used all these secret words," one girl chimed in, "words that only they knew. Jennifer told me that they had made them up, but I think they were taught them."

And this is how my words led to the death of the only other Bromely child, how I ended up killing both of them in a single day, one of which I deeply regret, the other of which I feel persistently ambivalent.

three mothers

There were three of them, dressed in black, sitting together on a branch at the top of a hemlock just east of the schoolyard, watching us children very closely. I could feel their gaze, could feel their eyes dividing me into pieces, into cuts of meat, could feel their intentions, could feel their hunger. I looked around the yard and saw the other children as these three saw them, as cattle, as a feast of raw young flesh just waiting to be claimed. I felt what they felt, an overwhelming desire to lick these children from head to toe, to savor the feeling of them beneath my tongue, longing to boil them and slowly drink the broth, or to eat the meat straight from the bone, pulling it off in strands, one limb at a time, each wound tied off to keep the beasts fresh, to keep them from dying due to blood loss and then beginning to rot before I could get my fill. In that moment I knew what they knew, could access their memories as if they were my own—I knew their names, where they lived, how they had become what they became—but just as quickly as it all came rushing in it left me, like a wave breaks on the shore and then returns to the ocean, and when I looked back to the hemlock they were gone, and since I was the only one who saw them, it was as if they had never been there to begin with.

the woman who could see

She was standing in the street as we made our way towards the school, her body shaking, her thin frame unable to deal with the sudden drop of temperature that winter brings, completely unprepared for cold weather now that none of her clothes fit right anymore, the fabric hanging loosely from her bones, providing next to no warmth at all. She was unmarried, this fact made obvious from her full head of hair—stringy, oily, unwashed for quite some time—her deathly thin silhouette, and her deep, sunken, bloodshot eyes.

One of the children called out to her, this woman, this neighbor or a friend of his mother's, to try and see what was the matter.

"Ms. Stockholm, are you okay? You shouldn't be out here like this. It's freezing."

She just stood and stared.

I started towards her, thinking I might guide her home, but then I saw the scissors in her hand and figured that she was just waiting for someone to try and touch her, longing to plunge the blades into the throat of some foolish young man who might think it respectful to walk a woman to her door, out to get revenge against the boys that never courted her when she was young and pretty and should have gotten married.

There were no other children foolish enough to get close to her, the scissors in her hand now obvious to us all, so we just watched her from afar, staring at her as she stared at nothing, her teeth gritted, determined to do something, but what exactly we could not say.

"Ms. Stockholm! Do you need help with something?"

"I want," she said, "to sleep."

Other adults started to come out of their houses, mostly men, some of the pregnant women, but only one or two of the other skinny spinsters, all of them ignoring us children, focused only on the woman with the scissors and the vacant stare.

"Every day is the same," she said, "no hunger, no tiredness, no physical urges of any kind. I just sit and stare, sit and stare, hoping for something to change, for desire to strike me, for a reason behind my life to present itself, but no, nothing, I just sit and stare and that's it, the hours turning into days, the days into months..."

She started laughing.

"I just realized that I don't know what day it is! I don't even know what month it is! How long have I been like this? How long have I felt nothing?"

The other skinny women went back into their homes, either driven back by depression, from the stark realities of which this woman spoke, or perhaps out of boredom, as uninterested in life as this woman claimed to be.

"I just want to sleep."

The woman lifted the scissors and scraped out her left eye, dragging the blades slowly, over and over, and then the right, and then dropped her hand to her side.

No one spoke up or ran to stop her.

Everyone just watched.

"I can still see," she yelled out, an unnatural laughter bubbling out of her as blood ran down her cheeks. "I can still see! Ha ha ha ha ha! I can still see!"

She dropped the scissors to the ground and put her hands up in the air.

"Take me to the tree of despair! Drag me to the bottom of the lake! Burn my body in the middle of the woods! Just let me sleep! All I want to do is sleep! I can still see! Oh god, why can I still see? I can still see everything! Just let me sleep! Just please, someone, let me sleep!"

I started towards school, unable to take any more of this woman, but I heard later that day, with the help of an axe and a willing set of hands, that Ms. Stockholm got her wish.

the prophecy

We were congregated at Raleigh's, there, as always, to gather information from the dead.

"You come to me for glimpses of the future," he said, "and you often leave disappointed, but today I have something you can sink your teeth into. I will be murdered before sundown. This is a fact. The one who kills me you will all know to be a sinner, and one of the few truly responsible for the hardships that have plagued this town, but you will let this person walk away from my corpse as if he has done something noble."

The men began to murmur, talking under their breaths, most of them unaware that they were making any noise at all.

"Already you dislike what I am saying. You must have caught that I said 'he'. The men in this town are not without guilt, in fact most of it belongs to them and them alone. The wolves want nothing from your children, and they never have. You murder them for no reason—that is when you are not molesting them, or leaving them to die in the darkness of the woods. Your wives are sinners, yes, and they are being punished—for their jealousy, for their pettiness—but most of their plight is to punish you, your women ugly so you will feel no desire, no inkling of ownership, so that you can not brag about them, or treat them as possessions, so you must think of them as people or not at all. Most of you have chosen not at all. This curse, though yours, is not just about you, but has been building for generations. Everything you have ever known in life has been a part of this curse, and it ends with you, and it ends in blood."

Raleigh smiled.

"Look at yourselves, look at each other. See the hatred burning behind the eyes of the men standing next to you. Almost every man in this room wants to kill me right now, but you are afraid of what it will look like, of what you would be admitting to. You are planning to come back later, alone, to confess transgressions before you bring about my death, to get your sins out in the open, off of your chest. You have felt a great burden since you let your wife and her friends murder the priest, feel weighed down by the things you've done to your own progeny, and you want these sins lifted—but more than that you want to stop my breath, to stop me from speaking against you in front of your fellow man. Let's not wait. Listen and I will give you permission to kill me now, to look like a hero. I was never kidnapped, never stolen away. I went to the wolves, ran to them, because I knew that they would not harm me. The dead had warned me long ago that you were the ones to fear, that you would be the ones to hand me over to the darkness of death. I came back only to find a picture of my wife, now dead eight years, because I missed her face, had begun to forget what she looked like, but my house had been ransacked since I'd left, and the picture I wanted was stolen, so I lit a candle and began to search for another, which is when you came and found me. I have never helped you since I have been your prisoner, telling you only what you wanted to hear, telling you that it was your wives and children who brought this curse, hoping that if I were to validate the sins you were already committing, if I were to approve of your wickedness, that you might turn me loose, but that was cowardly, and I was punished for my weakness of character, held here with you, trapped in this dreadful little town. I went to the wolves, and I would go back if I could. I told them all about you when I was there, where you live, what you do, who you hate, and they used it against you. I betrayed you, and it felt wonderful to do so, to have a hand in your misery. I wish I could see the wolves again. I have so much more to say to them, so many stories to tell. Like Howard, I would love to tell them what you did to your little Geraldine before dragging her to the forest... Do you remember that?"

Howard said nothing, just stared at the floor.

"She talks to me you know. They all do. They've told me about you. About all of you." Raleigh grinned and got to his feet. "Benjamin, my friend, are you ready to end this? Or do I need to tell these men about your fondness for Benjamin junior to get a proper reac..."

It happened fast and then over and over and over again

all at once, was like watching a thunderstorm reflected in the fragments of a broken mirror, seeing the men follow Benjamin's lead, hitting Raleigh again and again, together but separately, the same action repeated but with a different result every time. It took almost five minutes before the men realized what they were doing, that they were proving him right with every swing, validating his accusations, but by then it was far too late, the man a bloodied mass of flesh, not even recognizable as human. But he was breathing, the poor bastard still alive somehow, maybe even awake considering the way he was moving, but his face was too vandalized to tell one way or the other.

My father said, "What have we done," though he never threw a single punch, my old man knowing better than to single himself out, willing to admit to the sins of other men as not to seem above them.

"We can't leave him like this," Benjamin said, the man out of breath, almost in tears—not from regret but from the leftover adrenaline. "It is inhumane to leave him. We are better than this."

"I'll do it," said Carlton, Matthew's father and my own father's closest friend. "He claimed that the man who kills him would be a sinner, but we will prove him wrong."

Someone in the crowd handed him a knife.

"I will end this man's life—not out of hatred, but out of mercy, and respect, and as a gesture to the gods, to the wolves, letting them know that we hold no grudges against our fellow man, that we would do anything to spare him from the pain and agony of a slow death."

In one motion it was over, and, to my disgust, there was applause.

On the walk home I told my father, "That man killed both of his children, and we watched him kill his wife."

"I know," my father said. "And now we've seen him murder the only decent man I have ever known."

"We should leave this town, father."

"The curse is mine, son. It would follow me anywhere I chose to go."

We walked the rest of the way in silence, together and alone all at once.

the first

It first happened with Madeline, a younger girl, only nine, coming up to me at recess, cautiously, wincing slightly, acting as if I might be hot to the touch.

"I dream about you," she whispered. "And others, but always you. Are you afraid of the wolves?"

"No," I said, wanting to tell her that I dreamt of her too, but afraid of what might happen should someone overhear us.

"They mean you no harm. None of us need worry of their intentions. The curse is generational. It ends with our parents. The wolves will help us if we let them."

I nodded, unsure of what else to do.

"Do you know my name?"

"Madeline."

"How do you know that?"

I had never talked to her before, and didn't know her parents, and we had never shared a classroom or a mutual friend.

"I don't know."

"I do," she said, and then she walked away, yelling at another girl and starting to give chase, acting as though they were lost in an ongoing game of tag.

the second

And then it happened again a few days later.

Moses, a boy two years behind me, came up and sat beside me in the classroom we were forced to share—the class sizes continuing to shrink and grow as teachers and students disappeared or killed themselves—and halfway through a history lesson that was barely being taught the boy handed me a note on a piece of paper just a bit smaller than my palm.

DESTROY THIS.

I SEE YOU WHEN I SLEEP. WE MEET IN
THE WOODS, YOU AND ME AND
SEVERAL OTHERS, AND WE SIT, AND WE
SPEAK, AND WE CALL OUT TO THE

SPIRITS, AND THEY ANSWER US.
THEY TELL US WHAT TO DO, BUT IN
THE DREAM WE CAN'T HEAR THEM.
DO YOU WANT TO HEAR WHAT THEY
HAVE TO SAY? BECAUSE I DO, AND
SO DO THE OTHERS.

DESTROY THIS. DESTROY THIS.
DESTROY THIS. DESTROY THIS.

I shoved the note into my mouth and swallowed it without chewing. I knew the plan without asking him. That night, when there was a break in the clouds and the moonlight washed the soil in a moment of illumination, we would all leave our beds, climb out of our windows and walk into the woods, heading towards the mountains that housed the wolves we were all of us told to fear and hate.

sins of the youth

There had been a child hanged for drawing a picture on her desk, the image depicting three women standing shoulder to shoulder, their faces hidden in shadow, their bodies shapely, their hair full, their fingers long and thin. The girl's teacher, and soon after the principal, and eventually her parents, all felt that her drawing was a spell, a way to summon these women, and so they strung her up, hoping to stop her curse as they stopped the beating of her heart.

There was a child who was stoned to death for singing as he walked home, not by his parents, but by other children. He was singing a song that none of the children had heard before, and these children convinced themselves that it was the music of lost souls, the words being whispered to him by the devil, and so they began to attack the boy, determined to put a stop to it. Michelle, an older girl, started to speak on the boy's behalf, claiming him to be creative, saying that he was likely just making it up to entertain himself, but when the rocks began to fly her way she shut her mouth and hurried home.

There was a child that was drowned for bringing home a wounded bird. His parents thought nothing of it at first, but then his sister, driven to hysteria from a year of horror and tragedy, accused the boy of witchcraft and claimed that the bird was his familiar. She was ignored in the beginning, told not to speak against her brother, but then she began to screech, yelling over and over again that the boy was guided by darkness, and the bird, sensitive to sound, leapt from the boy's hands despite its wounded wings and flew out an open window. When asked how the bird could suddenly fly the boy had no answer, and so his father dragged him to the lake just after sunset and attempted to wash away his sins.

Still, we climbed out of our windows when the moon broke through, walked to the forest, and congregated.

and so it begins

There were nine of us, just as there had been in my dreams, Michelle being the last to join us as we marched into the woods. We stayed silent as we walked, no need for conversation, our feelings in the air, all of us calm, comfortable, and convinced that we were where we needed to be. We went deeper into the forest than we had ever been, but it all seemed familiar, as if we had been raised between the trees, as if they were all we knew, and when we found the clearing we had seen in our visions we all sat without saying a word, guided by instinct, as if pulled by invisible tethers. The words came, as we knew they would, but the language itself didn't matter, meant nothing to us, the incantation flowing through us, chaperoned by ancient spirits, the words just vessels for the intentions of the dead.

A fire began in the space between us, hot, bright, almost pure white heat with just hints of yellow and orange, and in the flame we saw images of the past.

There was a ceremony, long ago, in which the townspeople, the early settlers, gathered to honor their gods, to honor the wolves, the main source of their strength. The ritual was like none we had ever seen, full of joy and laughter, the men and women dressed in their best clothing, many of the children dressed as wolves themselves, everyone dancing and shouting to the heavens, thankful for a year of good fortune. All of a sudden the townspeople grew silent, began to stare off into the darkness, alert but not quite frightened as three wolves approached, the middle one the size of a moose, heavy, it seemed, with child. The crowd made room for the wolves to join them, and then circled around the beasts, while the priest of their time—a short man with a thick chestnut beard and the smallest tuft of hair on his large round skull—stood at the edge of the circle, smiling at the wolves and at his congregation, a slight smugness in his smirk that revealed to us that he had predicted this and that no one had believed him. The wolves lay down in the circle, the smaller ones on either side, their legs tucked beneath them, their heads up, alert, watching the crowd, while the large one rolled onto her back and began to push, her body going into labor. The crowd was terrified. They had been told that this would happen, said that they had been looking forward to it, eager to interact with the gods, a physical representation of the faith they had been born into, but to see the wolf before them frightened these people in a way that they had never even imagined possible, the foundations of their beliefs and their hold on reality shaken fiercely. Our town, as it turns out, was not a town of faith. Their religion, though embraced by nearly everyone in the town, was not taken literally, was not driven by spiritual devotion but rather as an expression of ritual, guided by a fear of change and growth. The wolf lying before them, not a wolf at all but something more, was a nightmare come to life, a monster they had never considered to actually walk the earth, and yet here it was, giving birth to some unknown beast, and they, according to scripture, were supposed to feel blessed to witness such a thing. The priest began to mutter the sacred words, and the large wolf let out a howl that sounded more like the scream of a woman, then collapsed into the afterlife as a human girl with copper hair crawled out from the wolf's nethers, the girl pale, cloaked in freckles, with small, soft, but pronounced breasts and a tuft of pubic hair between her legs, born at the age of thirteen, already sexually mature. This was the goddess of the wolves, the wolfmother, born again after hundreds of years of death, ready to lead her pack to their promised salvation, happy to bestow blessings on the humans who would help her achieve this, but this night, so long ago, was not the beginning of such things. The wolfmother was struck with a club, the blow knocking her down to her knees, and the two remaining wolves attacked the man who had swung the stick, while several other men pulled knives, broke bottles, and went after these noble beasts, the sight of their blood the men's only desire. The women began to grab their children and flee the scene, as the priest—horrified by the actions of his congregation—began to try and pull his men from the wolves but then was struck down himself, knocked unconscious. Soon the wolves were dead, and all that was left was the girl—still alive but slightly dazed from being struck—and the men, seething with bloodlust. As it turned out, it was not fear that made the first man swing his club, but desire; his longing to destroy the young woman, to steal her innocence, to use her until she died. This girl, she was beautiful, not only the shape of her but also the light that she held within, and the man's corrupt heart could not stand to be in the presence of something so divine and not have it for himself.

And this man, of course, was not the only one.

The men did terrible things to this girl, one after another, until the priest awoke and saw what was happening. Being the only man who knew the consequences of such vile actions, the priest took a knife that had been abandoned on the ground and lunged at the girl, at the great goddess he had waited his whole life to meet, and drove the blade deep into her heart, killing the young woman but sparing her from further pain and torture. Her body began to dry up instantly, burning from within, and in a few moments there were only ashes left where the wolfmother once lay.

And thus, our town was cursed.

seven of seven

We left the forest one by one, our hearts heavy with regret, with guilt passed down, inherited from the actions of our parents and their parents before them. Every generation since the one that killed the wolfmother had committed a similar sin, some horrific crime against nature that the whole town covered up, keeping the curse alive, helping it run its course, leading to the horrors that we were facing each and every day.

"The last generation will suffer the most," Michelle said right before she left the clearing in the woods and started home, quoting from our visions, the words of a wise woman two generations after the original crime who was eventually burned at the stake for being a witch; for telling the townspeople things that they didn't want to hear. "This, like all things, will end in blood."

We had seen hundreds of individual moments in the forest that night, spanning all six generations of the curse, including the crime each generation committed to start the cycle all over again, the most recent, of course, being the murder of the young couple and their newborn daughter. We watched the men approach the house, drunk, angry, afraid more than anything but leaning on each other for strength. There were seven men total, including Carlton, Matthew's father, and Bartholomew, the father of Eloise, the one who killed his daughter twice. We watched the men force their way into the home, watched them attack the young man first, breaking his left leg, several of his ribs, and then his jaw, then making him watch as they ravaged his wife, one after another, each man taking at least one turn, and most of them a second. We watched as the men grabbed this young woman by the arms and legs and pulled her to pieces, one man standing on her chest to keep her steady, the strength of these men almost superhuman, the girl's flesh ripping apart like wet cloth. We watched these men as they nailed the poor child to the wall, watched them cut her scalp and then place it in the father's mouth just before they took out their blades and made his body match his wife's. We watched these men congratulate each other, talking about the child as if she were a witch, a spawn of Satan, citing the scripture all of us knew that warned of red-headed women, warned of their unnatural powers, of their unearthly abilities.

We watched the men leave drunk, no longer affected by the booze they had consumed but rather drunk on violence, on the level of control you feel when you take someone's life away from them. This feeling of power is what eventually led one of these men, a Heathcliff, the husband of my mother's friend, to strangle his only son in a fit of rage, the same child that I was asked to pose with for a picture, the child who was said to have died from a fit, or from a spell of heat. This is what led another of these men to drown his wife out on the lake, telling friends and neighbors that she had fallen out of their boat on accident, and that it was her clothes—too many layers, too heavy—soaking up water that had caused her to go beneath the surface and not return until all of her breath was gone for good. Every one of these men would kill once more before the curse would start anew, which ended with Carlton, the last of the seven men to commit a private act of murder.

It was the day before the wolves came down, late in the afternoon, the sun just getting ready to set. Carlton was with a young woman, an Allison, much younger than himself, still just a child, only fifteen years old and living at home with her parents. The two of them were in her father's barn, tucked away behind some tools and a few old crates, making love quietly, both of them aware of what would lay in store for them if they were to be found out. They had been seeing each other for a few weeks, ever since Allison had been sent to Carlton's farm by her father to deliver a bottle of milk, a gift from the one man to the other in the hopes that they might start a partnership, something Allison's father had been pressuring Carlton to do for several weeks by that point. Carlton had seen the girl a thousand times and thought nothing of her, but that first afternoon, the air warm, the sun high in the sky and beating down, Allison had a glisten to her that she had never before shown in his presence, and looked, in that moment, like a full-grown woman instead of the child he had always known her to be.

"Is the milk cold?" he asked her, smiling, not taking it from her hands as she held it out.

"As cold as ice."

"Well then let's split it," he said, "because you look parched," and then he guided her to the shade of a tree. As he had suggested, the two shared the cold beverage, and then moments later their own warm bodies.

From that first afternoon they had made it a point to see each other at least once or twice a week, him thrilled to be in the arms of a woman that was not his wife, her excited to be acknowledged as a woman at all, and it was on one such afternoon, in her father's barn the day before the wolves descended, that they were caught in the act.

Allison's father was a wealthy man, as prosperous as anyone else in the town, and with a large field of crops he had the need for extra hands, so he had hired several teenage boys—too old for school but still young enough that they weren't married with a house and family of their own. Jeremiah was one such young man, a baker's son, handsome with hay-colored hair and a small gap in his front teeth, who only took the job because he had for years been in love with Allison, the fabled beautiful and charming "boss's daughter." It proved to be this foolish crush that got him killed, because though he knew from the sounds that he had heard what was happening in the barn, it was out of his love for Allison that he had to investigate. Try as he did, Jeremiah could not fight the urge to see his favorite woman beneath this other man, because he, like most romantic fools, secretly longed to have his heart broken. He didn't yell at the couple, or call the young woman any hurtful names for following the longings of her young, changing body, but instead said only one word, just her name, half-whispered, the boy on the verge of tears.

"Allison..."

And Carlton, mid-thrust, heard this and jumped to his feet, grabbed the young man by the shirt and slammed his fist into him so hard that the boy instantly lost consciousness. The girl cried out, not in fear or repulsion but in excitement, proud that her soft body could lead a man to violence, that she was something to be fought over.

"You know you have to kill him," she whispered, reaching out and grabbing Carlton's member, still exposed and full of blood, and after the job was done, the boy's heart no longer beating, Carlton returned to the young woman and picked up where they had left off, knowing that it would be best to wait until after sundown before they tried to move the body.

Then the next day came the wolves, and the curse, and the priest's declaration that it was a child who brought the vicious creatures down from the mountain.

Three guesses as to which young woman was the first to go missing.

the boogeyman

Moses and I were sitting on the grass late one morning, glad to be away from our respective households. Like me, Moses had recently lost a close friend, the child murdered in the name of the curse, and so Moses had been stuck at home with his family, unwilling to go out and play on his own, aware of the consequences that the perception of him as a "lone wolf" would provide. Now that we had a reason to leave the house, Moses and I began to spend nearly all of our free time together, excited to once again have someone that we could trust. In truth we wanted to spend our time with all of the children that had come together in the forest that night, but large numbers were just as dangerous as single children in the eyes of the adults, and so to keep ourselves safe we mostly paired off, choosing a child or two and keeping them company.

"We used to catch fireflies," Moses told me, speaking of his friend Zachary, the boy who had been taken from him just a few weeks before, while I showed him how to make a boat out of paper. "We would keep them in mason jars, and hold onto them as long as we could. We had talked ourselves out of feeling guilty for keeping them trapped since we would carry them around with us wherever we would go, which we considered similar to flight, but this ill logic only held so long before I wised up and released the insects. Zachary became obsessed with bugs though, and would catch them and pin them to wood. He wasn't cruel, would not catch and kill any bug he saw, but simply one from each species, or a male and a female if there was a difference between the sexes."

"I tried to collect rocks once," I said while folding another boat, "but it couldn't hold my interest."

"I was the same way with leaves. I just don't have the passion for it. But Zachary found something in the bugs, though I wish he hadn't. I'm sure that if it hadn't been his collection his father would have found another reason to kill him, but as it stands the boy was accused of using the pinned bodies as a way to control the feelings of others, as ludicrous as you and I know that to be."

"Any reason they can find," I said.

"Any reason at all."

The afternoon carried on, and so did conversation. We tried to play with the boats we made, pretending that they carried sailors from distant lands, but with all we had been through it was hard to see the value in it. We were getting ready to call it a day when a sudden uproar of voices manifested a few streets away, and with nothing better to do we followed the ruckus to a find a crowd of people dragging a man from his home, yelling at him and cursing his name, a sight so commonplace that we considered leaving without gathering the details, but our curiosity got the best of us.

"It seemed like such a waste!" the man hollered from the ground, kicking and thrashing and trying to break free. "I was out to honor them!"

The man was a widower, his wife murdered months before, the holder of the short straw on the day that they decided to cut a pregnant woman open. It took a few minutes to piece together the situation, but apparently the man, a Jameson, had decided to keep his wife's body rather than dispose of it, preserving the woman with salts and various chemicals of his own concoction. He claimed to have loved the woman, didn't want to live without her, and so he turned her corpse into a shrine, her body propped in a chair and decorated with candles and pieces of silver, dried spices and lengths of chain. But once he started he decided that his wife's body was not enough and soon began to frequent the graveyard, pulling up bodies from the shallow graves that families barely even bothered to dig, bringing the corpses home to make individual pieces—a human torso with three hands sewn in where the head shoud be, a stack of salted tongues on a long and slender piece of metal—or to further build on his original shrine, something that had grown far beyond a simple gesture to his wife.

All of this was confessed in short bursts between bouts of violence, the man at this point tied by his neck and ankles to a tree on the edge of the forest.

"But what about my son?" Carlton said. "Why do you have my son in there?"

"Matthew..." I whispered and shot Jameson's house a glance, then looked back at the man, my full attention finally granted.

"And my daughter?" a woman added.

"And my two boys?" asked another.

"I found them..." the man said, working for every breath, "in the forest... where you left them..."

"Where I left him?" Carlton bellowed. "I did not leave my son anywhere! He was stolen from me! Taken from his bed in the night!"

I had to cover my mouth to keep from shouting, from reminding the crowd that this man had admitted to killing both his son and his daughter, to the whole town, not six weeks earlier, moments before killing his own wife, but they knew as well as I did, and this new lie was simply more appealing.

"And my daughter!" cried out another woman, possibly the mother of Eloise, but of course all the mothers looked the same. "You stole my daughter from me!"

"I never stole... a single child... I just took... them in..."

The crowd kept going around and around about all of the crimes this man had committed, pinning every sin they could think of onto him—every molested child, every murdered spouse—but he just continued talking, trying to explain that what he had been doing was a good thing.

"I just wanted them... to be loved... again... I wanted them... to be beautiful..."

The truth, though vile enough, was unimportant—what the crowd wanted was a scapegoat, the body of a man to accept punishment for all of the crimes that they had commited. Moses and I stayed as long as we could stomach, but when a hammer was produced the both of us turned and walked away, moving quickly, neither of us speaking a word.

a natural conclusion

My sister came to me in the middle of the night. We had been talking more than usual, sometimes spending as much as three hours together each day, just sitting in a room and tending to our hobbies, or playing quietly with a deck of cards. Most of her friends had gone missing at that point, and with our mother completely unapproachable and our father afraid to get too close to my sister as beautiful as she was, uncertain of how his body would react if he put himself in a questionable situation, Megan was rather lonely indeed.

"Wake up," she said, touching my hair. "I can't sleep again."

I sat up in my bed, unsure of what she meant with this declaration. She had never expressed an inability to sleep, though considering what her life had become, it was more than understandable.

I said, "I don't sleep so well myself these days," which was true, but only because I had been choosing, at least one or two nights a week, to return to the forest with the other children, to see the things that the spirits cared to show us, to try and find a way to ensure that our generation would not make the same mistakes the others had.

"I just... I can't stop thinking about you," she touched my hair again, caressed my face, "and how sweet you've been to me lately..."

My mind flashed to the demons that the men spoke of, the ones tied to us from birth, the ones we gather with our sins to pass down to the children that we bring into the world, the ones that we build upon one another until we are constantly suffocating. Though I believed in next to nothing that the elders spoke of, I suddenly wondered if their beliefs, at one point, had some grounding in reality. Would I be tarnishing myself if I accepted what was obviously a sexual advance from my older sister? Could anything we do consensually to one another be anything like a sin? Or was there something neccessary in two sad and lonely people comforting one another with their bodies, something beautiful that transcended what was deemed inappropriate or unholy by anyone outside of the moment?

I took my sister's hand, pulled it from my face, held onto it for just a moment, and then released it, pulled away. In the end, the truth came easy.

"I love you dearly, and you know that, but stuff like this will get us killed."

She nodded, looked away, sure that I was right.

"I'm just so lost," she said. "And I don't know what else to do."

"It's okay," I said to her, "I can see how it came to this," but she was up and walking to the door, embarrassed and frustrated and longing to be anywhere other than next to me.

In the morning, at breakfast, my sister wouldn't look at me, and her distance carried through the schoolday, through the afternoon, the evening, the week, the month, and so on. From that moment, from the rejection of her body, my sister, my dear Megan, acted as if I had never even existed.

the animal feast

I was sitting with Moses, leaning against an old hemlock near the center of town, watching the other children play, the two of us in near silence, communicating with our eyes, with our expressions, speaking volumes with pursed mouths and worried looks. Moses had first noticed our problem a few moments after school let out, sitting on the grass outside of our classroom, waiting for me to gather my things, when a gaggle of young girls walked between him and the building, six girls in total and only five shadows cast. He hopped up and followed the girls, making sure that his eyes were not just playing tricks on him, but when he walked after them he saw that there was one girl, a Gretchen, nine years old, who was living without a shadow.

"Gretchen has no shadow," he whispered to me when I finally caught up with him.

"I'm sorry, but I don't know who Gretchen is."

He nodded towards a short, dark-haired girl in a white dress, dancing and laughing with her friends.

"What do we do?" he asked.

I shrugged.

"Nothing. You remember what happened last time, and of course, the time before that."

There had been only one child since Jennifer—a young boy by the name of Kenneth—who we had discovered to not have a shadow. It was Lillian who first noticed, because she and Kenneth sat next to each other in class, friendly with one another, smiling and making jokes when they could get away with it, attracted to each other in the way that young children sometimes are. She was looking at Kenneth, trying to get his attention so that he would take a folded note, when she saw the desk beneath his arm and realized that it was covered evenly with light, his arm not an obstruction, the rays passing through him as if he were made of glass. Determined not to draw any attention to him, Lillian pulled her eyes away and focused on her teacher, her own desk, anything but her friend and his missing shadow.

Lillian turned to us for advice when she saw us at half break, and Michelle suggested that we simply let the boy know of his misfortune, so that he might prepare himself and hopefully stay protected from harm. Lillian was reluctant to tell him, asking one of us to take her place, but we knew that he would feel threatened if anyone else were to point it out, that it had to be her or no one at all, though to convince her to go through with it Moses and I had to agree to accompany her as moral support.

When Lillian told Kenneth of his situation there was a reaction, but nothing as dramatic as we had anticipated, the boy somber yet accepting, as if he had been waiting for such a thing to happen. We told him that we would try and help him, that we would gather supplies so that he could leave the next morning before school, so he could run away to a place that might be more forgiving, or better yet, where no one would notice, and then he just thanked us and went home, walking slowly, obviously shaken. The next morning we took our supplies—food, a compass, a few books and a small pad of paper—but Kenneth never arrived at school, the boy gone missing a day before schedule. Whether he got anxious and ran off early, or perhaps was slain by his parents after giving himself away, unable to keep himself together as the day turned into night, we would never know for sure, but we had our suspicions.

And thus, Moses and I, our backs against a tree near the middle of town, had no course of action, nothing we could do for poor Gretchen but to sit and wait and see what happened. It was nerve-wracking, watching Gretchen jump rope with the other girls, just waiting for one of them to notice her missing shadow as they watched her feet leave the ground, but it never came, the girls too focused on the number of jumps, too wrapped up in their competition to notice anything else, which included Gretchen's mother, storming in from the north with her husband, a hand full of drawings and a small following of townsfolk, all of them with fire in their eyes.

"Gretchen, you devil!" her mother yelled, snatching the girl from her game and throwing her to the ground. "You beast! You rotten little thing!"

Her father removed his belt and began to strike the girl with the buckle side, repeatedly, about the face and torso, large gashes splitting open, blood everywhere.

"You cursed us! You brought this upon your father and me! You cursed everyone!"

The man stopped swinging his belt and his wife held out the pages for the crowd to see, drawings the girl had apparently done, most of which I could not make out from my distance, but I did catch a glimpse of one, a drawing of animals—mostly wolves with a few horses and owls thrown in—dressed as men and women, sitting down together to share a great meal. The woman turned back to her daughter, pushing the drawings against the girl's face.

"Is this what you want?" she screamed, her words barely comprehensible. "For us to be replaced by these beasts? For them to live in our homes and sleep in our beds?"

The girl's father wrapped his belt around his daughter's neck and began to drag her away, to leave her to die in the woods like all the rest of them.

Moses and I both realized in that moment, without either of us needing to say it out loud, that the missing shadow was not necessarily a curse but a sort of blessing, an advance warning of who would be next to meet their end.

As Gretchen was taken away we made our way into the crowd to speak ill of the child, to show our support for her parents and what they did, to blend in as much as possible.

As the crowd dispersed we too left, eager to blend in as much as possible, to keep our shadows where they belonged.

the miracle of birth

Not long after our night in the woods there was a woman, the wife of a man I didn't know, who went into labor just as soon as morning broke, as the sun was coming up behind the clouds. She, like all the other women, had been pregnant for just over fourteen months, convinced that she would stay that way until death carried her away from the life that she hardly knew anymore. Word spread quickly through the village, and we gathered in front of the woman's home, worried for her life, half expecting someone to kill her before she could even have the child, our town at the point where murder was the answer to nearly every new development. I was able, with the help of my father, to push my way inside the house and see the woman for myself. She was naked, on the bed not in it, struggling alone with the labor, no one willing to get close enough to help her or to hold her hand, afraid of what might be coming out of this woman. There was talk of various possibilities—snakes, wolves, darkness—but what they feared the most was a child. If a child came out, whose would it be? Should they kill it for fear of the devil? Or could it be one of their gods come into the flesh of man, ready to lead them to salvation? And if that was the case, how could they stop one of these other men from killing it? These known child murderers that walked among us, too well-liked to be charged for their crimes—how could they be stopped? But the fears of a child were unfounded, as it was maggots and flies and rotten meat that escaped from this woman, her insides coming out decayed, broken down, the flesh obviously dead for weeks at least, possibly months, and when we looked back to her face we saw only thin skin held loosely to a slack-jawed skull, her eyes missing, rotted out, and we realized that this woman had been walking around dead, her body swollen with decomposition, flies and other insects feasting on her corpse. For months this woman had tended to her children, spent time with her husband, and worked in the garden as a dead woman, her soul trapped in a worthless body, everyone around her unable to see the truth that was staring them in the face. She was not giving birth, but rather her body was finally releasing her soul, the rot catching up quickly, making up for lost time. Women screamed in terror, their husbands speechless, too shocked to even respond with violence, and the children led the evacuation, everyone leaving the poor man to remove his wife's remains alone, uninterested in helping him deal with the tragedy that could potentially strike every other family in town within a few short hours, or, just as likely, no one else at all.

brothers and sisters

I awoke in the dead of night and felt compelled to go into the woods, so I slipped on my shoes and climbed out through the window, joining the others, all of them pulled as I had been out from a dead sleep.

There were nine of us—Moses and Fredderick, both age twelve, two years younger than myself, Michelle, two years older, Olivia, age thirteen, Lillian and Jeremiah, both age eleven, Madeline age nine, and Samuel who was fourteen like me—and I, of course, made nine. Most of us had not been friends before our visions, but since they had begun we found that we had no real interest in any of the other children. However, to avoid suspicion we had to stay apart as much as possible, to pretend like our interactions in public were meaningless and a matter of circumstance. There was no explaining why a fourteen year old boy like myself or Samuel would be interested in carrying on a lengthy conversation with Madeline—perhaps the most gifted of us children, her visions often probing deeper than the rest of us could go—so we could only ever give her a little wave or a brief hello before moving along, when in actuality we wanted to sit and talk away the afternoon with her. But in the forest we could engage Madeline, and Lillian, and Fredderick, brilliant young people who were able to see so clearly what the rest of us were blind to.

We walked through the woods together, holding hands, all of us very fond of one another and eager to show our affection through this simple gesture. We arrived in the clearing, as we always did, drawn to this same spot, and sat, our hands still held, waiting for the words to come and bring the fire; to bring the visions; to bring the truth. But the words never came. We sat, waiting, our eyes closed, but nothing. We opened our eyes and looked around the circle at one another and realized that the wolves had not pulled us into the forest this night, but that we had in fact called upon one another ourselves, had wanted to see each other, and so subconsciously we drove each other out of our beds one by one.

We had come together simply to be ourselves.

That night we spoke of our lives, of our parents, of our pasts. We spoke of the wolves, and of the other children, and of the future. We told each other jokes, and fables, and laughed—as children will—at absolutely nothing. We had become a family and we hadn't even realized it. We made our way back into our beds just before sunrise, not rested but energized, alive in a way that we had not been in quite some time.

the dark room

There was a crowd of children gathered as I walked into the main hallway of the schoolhouse, the kids grouped tightly together, silent, fixated on something that I apparently couldn't see. I approached Moses, standing near the back of the crowd, and asked him what was going on.

"The door to Ms. Hubble's room is ajar, just a crack, and we don't know who opened it."

I looked up ahead at the classroom door and saw the sliver of darkness, the room in fact open for the first time in months. I closed my eyes, hoping that something might come to me, that I might get some quick vision as to what lay in store, but no such thing was shown to me—all I had were memories of the last time I saw Ms. Hubble, the woman crying, sad to let us go, heartbroken to have to abandon us for solitude. I remembered her teeth, and how tall she had become, each limb easily eight feet long, if not longer, and those slits on her cheek and forehead. Whatever lay behind that door, no matter its intention, would not be pretty in the least.

Of course, there were children who wanted to investigate.

"We'll draw straws," said Abel, a stocky boy a bit older than me with a man's jaw and a receding hair line that made him look like he was going on thirty. "And the shortest one goes in."

"We don't have straws."

"Then we'll count potatoes."

We all held out our fists and Abel counted potatoes. There were a few of us there, the game taking a while, but I knew who would lose and what would happen to him, as did Moses, as did Lillian and Fredderick, because while Abel counted we looked at the children's feet, saw that David did not have a shadow, and concluded that he would be the next to die.

A hand was counted out, and then another, and the game continued.

"...seven potatoes more, one... big... bad... spud. That's both fists. You're out."

It turned out that it was not David as we had thought, but Danielle who was chosen to investigate, and since she still had a shadow we knew that she'd be safe. A wave of relief washed over me, comforted to know that Ms. Hubble was either friendly or dead, or perhaps the room was empty, the door left open from her escape.

Danielle swallowed her fear and began, slowly, to approach the door, not wanting to fight the decision, afraid of what might come of it, but as she got closer to the room she slowed to a crawl, and ended up stopping some ten feet away.

"I can't do this," she said, turning and running back. "I can't do this, I can't do this, I can't do this!"

"Hell," said David, "I'll do it," and before anyone could stop him he was at the door to Ms. Hubble's room, pushing it open as confidently as he might the front door of his house, and then we saw them, the six milky eyes floating there, not glowing but reflecting the light, and then two long, thin, grey and hairy legs grabbed onto David and pulled him into the room, the door closing back to just a thin strip of darkness, his screams quickly replaced by the hissing and clicking of large jaws full of teeth, for it seemed that with her transformation complete, Ms. Hubble had finally regained her appetite. Most of the children ran away screaming, but the ones who remained were instructed by Abel to fetch their fathers, to tell them to bring weapons and fire, except for Danielle who he had demanded stay with him.

"I want to go home!" she said, the girl crying like a widow.

"No, you did that on purpose. You knew what would happen, so you sent someone else to die in your place, and now you're going to answer for it. The men will need something to distract the beast before they go in to kill it, and I know just the girl."

She tried to get away but he held onto her hair, one arm twisted behind her back, a smile stretched across his face.

We looked at their feet for a shadow and could not find one for either child, both of them suddenly marked for death with this new turn of events. We left them in the hallway, uneager to watch them meet their fate, and went our separate ways, ignoring Abel's requests to call our fathers, knowing that he wouldn't be around to rat us out.

the congregation

I was sitting on the grass with Michelle and Olivia, watching the day go by, no school left to go to, the entire building burned down in the attempt to kill Ms. Hubble who just ended up escaping into the woods anyway, dragging two screaming men along with her into the darkness between the trees. It was early in the day, grey as always because of the clouds, but we were content to just sit and be simple, to take the day as it came, the three of us interested only in being close to one another. It had been a difficult couple of weeks, another child missing nearly every day, the threat against us increased without a school to go to, without someone to notice a child's absence, but we knew of their deaths, the nine of us, as we had been shown all of these murders in the visions that we could not escape.

Lying on the grass, Olivia began to tell us stories about

being young, about her mother and how close they had been, about the way that she would teach her everything—how to cook, how to sew, and would even help her with her studies, explaining math problems and sentence structure—but then how her mother had, since the curse first took effect, begun to shun Olivia, refusing to share anything, going silent every time the girl walked into a room.

"She acts as though I am her competition, as if I am out to steal what is hers. She treats me as though I am not her daughter, but rather like I am a younger version of herself, that she has been raising her replacement, and she hates me for it."

It was then—Olivia hearing her own words, realizing the truth behind the statement, suddenly aware that her mother did in fact hate her—that the first of the spinsters passed by, dressed in her Sunday best, walking with determination. It was Ms. Ferguson, a school teacher before the wolves, one of the first women to quit, driven mad from her inability to sleep. She had been known to sit in her house and yell, to scream for hours on end, but she knew when to stop, never going on so long or so late into the night that the men might gather together to help put the woman to bed. She looked good in her clothes—as good as such an ugly woman could look. She was skinny like the rest, but her clothes fit, must have been tailored down to wrap around her tiny frame. We watched as she went west, out to Ms. Holliday's house, another spinster, and walked in without knocking as if it were her own home. Then there was another one, and then another, these unwed women looking so put together, walking with dignity to their friend's house, letting themselves in, gathering perhaps as some sort of support group or reading circle, women with a shared grief drawn together just as us nine children had been by our visions, bound by something bigger than we were able to comprehend. Over the course of half an hour, nearly every unmarried woman in the town arrived at that house, showing up one at a time, never running up to walk with a friend or waiting up ahead for a woman to make pace, each of them coming alone as if on purpose. And then, suddenly, the house was on fire, catching quickly, obviously planned, and we watched as people came out from their homes to try and put it out before it spread, unaware of the women inside, the townspeople concerned only with themselves. We expected to see women running out of the building, women who had changed their minds and decided that they did not want to die, that as awful as life had become it was still better than nothing at all, but no, the door never opened, and no one tried to escape. The fire burned bright as if it were hotter than it should have been, consuming the house quite quickly, and then it went out all on its own. There was still plenty of wood left to burn, still air to keep it going, but the fire had finished what it had set out to do, and so, suddenly, as quickly as it began, it was over, and the women that the house contained were finally allowed to sleep.

flickering images of past and present

We had our own visions, each of us nine chosen children, and we would share them in the woods, circled around the fire, all of us chanting, seeing what the others saw.

We saw several men, some of our fathers but not mine, congregated together and speaking of the children, of the women, and of the curse. The men saw their own health as a sign of purity, not plagued by the curse but blessed with vitality, and so they began to discuss a mass murder of all the hideous wives, the thin spinsters, and all the male children, leaving only the beautiful daughters, so many in number that even with all the ones that had gone missing there would be enough left for each man to take and marry at least three, the polygamy not ideal, they said, but necessary to repopulate the town and carry on the faith as it should be taught. They made a list of all the girls, even the young ones, and began to divide them up among themselves, men promising away their own daughters in exchange for another man's, choosing only two a piece for the moment, leaving the rest of the girls to be fought over as more men came to join them. They decided that they would need more members to accept their specific interpretation of old scripture before they began the cleansing, or else they could be stopped by the few wicked men that were sure to be hidden among the righteous.

We saw women, bald and pregnant, standing over their children as they slept, the women's eyes appearing dead, unfeeling, a knife or an axe or a fire poker held in their hands, the women trying to will themselves to kill their wicked offspring, or, in some cases, trying to use the sight of their possibly innocent children as motivation to end their own lives, to save these children from themselves. Nearly every mother in town held this practice, so fed up with life as a perpetually pregnant, hideous creature that she would do almost anything to make it end, but most of these women were not the monsters they appeared to be, but rather women who still, on some level, felt like mothers. As vile and sinful as they suspected their children to be, these women still held a fondness for them and so they would not attack, just stand and stare, then give up and go to bed to toss and turn and wait for the torment of tomorrow.

We saw three women, shoulder to shoulder, always moving together, floating slightly, their toes hovering just above the ground, their faces hidden in darkness. These women were shapely, everything a woman should be, with hips and breasts, slightly pouty but smooth stomachs, their skin creamy and soft, unblemished, nearly hairless. These women dressed all in black, their dresses identical, immaculate, beautiful. We saw the cabin in which they lived, built from mud and straw on the side of a small hill, the front of it grown over with trees and moss, hidden unless you knew what you were looking for. The inside of the cabin was wallpapered in darkness, the stolen shadows of the dead spread across the walls, writhing for eternity in grief and unbearable, torturous pain, with the skin of murdered wolves pulled over wood to make furniture, a home decorated in the agony of others. We saw these three women drag children who had been abandoned in the forest back to this cabin, to lock them up next to all the others, a spell cast on the children's eyes so they could see nothing but the women, blind to those who surrounded them. We watched the women feed the children until it was time to feed themselves, choosing a child at random, eating everything—flesh, hair, teeth, bone—everything, that is, except the hands, which they nailed to the walls, positioning the fingers as if the dead children were casting spells, a ritual that protected the women from the wolves that longed to end their lives, the wolves that circled them and their cabin, waiting for their magic to grow weak and their bodies to become vulnerable to attacks.

We saw the wolves themselves, most of them waiting patiently in the mountains for something they knew would soon be on its way.

We saw the present and the past intertwined together, a tapestry of wicked deeds carried out in desperate moments, but we never saw the future anymore, nothing at all of things yet to come. Our future, it seemed, had yet to be written, our path still unclear, our souls not yet damned.

.

on a lake of blood and tears, in the forest of the damned

Raleigh came to see me once more, months after his death, just one week before I was banished, the man waiting for me in a dream. We were on a lake of tears and blood, floating in a boat made from woven hair, the woods around us built from the corpses of the damned, their bodies now trunks, their arms tree limbs, their fingers branches, the bodies returned to the earth now that their sinning was behind them.

"Raleigh," I said, "why did you let them do that to you? Why did you encourage them to end your life?"

"So that I would not become one of them."

Raleigh held out a piece of paper with a symbol scrawled

in red ink, fairly simple but unlike anything I had ever seen.

"This was given to me by the wolves to pass on to you. You are the only one who can wear it, for whom it will do any good. This was meant for you from the day you were born."

The drawing in his hand caught flame and burned away to ashes, but the image was clear in my mind, as vivid a concept as my own name.

When I woke up it was still dark out, would be for a while, so I took advantage of being alone and carved the symbol I had been shown into the meat of my upper thigh, using an old shirt as a bandage to stop the bleeding, hoping to hide this wound from the town, knowing that if anyone were to see it I would be strung up in the streets, but by sunrise the wound was closed with only the scar remaining, no pain to be felt, and I walked among the townspeople as if nothing had changed at all.

the red tide

The first one that I witnessed was the father of our late friend William, a man who was often present when things went wrong, a busybody without responsibility or purpose after he had murdered his wife and son in the name of the town. The man had been one of the first to accuse his own family of witchcraft, a pioneer in the paranoid savagery that had since become the rule, but he was one of few men who seemed to feel guilty for what he did, who would occasionally question the validity of his actions before forgoing his self-doubt and once again joining the town in viciousness.

The man was in the street near the empty lot where the church had once stood, staring at nothing, holding his stomach. He seemed off, but looked perfectly healthy, his color rich as if he had been touched by the sun every day, though it had only broken through the clouds a handful of times since the wolves had first come down some fifteen months before, and his hair was thick and dark like I had never seen it before the curse, the man almost bald back then, his remaining hair mostly white with a few hints of medium grey. And yet despite his fit body, something seemed wrong.

It was his eyes, I realized, that betrayed him, as they looked suddenly old, tired even beyond his years, and then, as I watched him, his mouth opened and blood began to move slowly down his chin, then a bit faster, the man beginning to retch, coughing it up with chunks of tissue, all of his insides seemingly escaping out from his mouth. But the man did not die, just kept moving the blood out from his body, a pretty steady flow, and then, suddenly, he stopped, wiped his mouth, and walked home as if nothing had happened.

He was not the only one, as it seemed that every man in the village was facing this same fate, some of them more violently, coughing up gargantuan amounts of blood, doubling over in pain, while others were only mildly affected, a little bit of blood, just a few mouthfuls coming out of them now and then. But every man seemed to be bleeding, even my father, a man I still saw as innocent.

The town was full of smiling women that night, and beautiful men with sad eyes, their bodies rotting from the inside out, these miserable men unable to die no matter how much blood they lost.

father, son

I was standing with Michelle beneath an old elm, watching her eat an apple, looking so intently that she began to laugh, her cheeks red, warm with the happiness that the moment provided.

"Would you like this apple for yourself?"

I smiled and shook my head.

"No, I just like to look at you, like to see the thoughts move across your face... But I would be interested in where you found it... I haven't see one of those in at least six months, probably closer to a year."

She smiled.

"Moses and Samuel found a tree, guided by a dream they both had. There were four apples, so they gave one to me, one to Madeline, and then both had one themselves."

I nodded and she laughed, sure to see the jealousy on my face.

"You can have a bite, honey. I'd be happy to share it with you."

I took the apple and kissed her cheek as if to thank her, but mostly just to kiss her, to feel her flesh beneath my lips, but when we touched a rush shot through the both of us with visions of a bloody bedroom, the body of a pregnant woman half on the bed, half off, her face hidden in the ruffle of the blankets.

I dropped the apple, turned and ran, called back an apology, told Michelle that I would make it up to her, that I would find another way to make her smile, but she had seen what I had seen, knew what I knew, and expected no form of compensation.

The house in the vision had been my own.

When I arrived home I found my father sitting on the porch, a bottle in his hand, drinking for perhaps only the second or third time since I had been born. He looked tired, both physically and mentally, and he was wet with what could only be blood.

"Your mother killed your sister," he said in a practiced but honest voice. "And then I killed your mother."

"What happened?"

"Your sister was at the table, sewing as usual, and your mother struck her three times with a frying pan, right in front of me, unprovoked. I grabbed a knife and stabbed your mother, because I didn't know what else to do. Twice. In the neck. Then I dragged her to the bedroom."

He stood quickly and threw the bottle hard against the front of our house, the glass shattering, liquor going everywhere, and he looked at me with tear-soaked eyes.

"And then you know what I did? I cut open her stomach just to see what I would find."

I couldn't help myself, I said, "What was in there?"

"Two dead rattlesnakes and the front half of a fox, the thing bleeding as if torn in two but still alive, the back half nowhere to be found. I killed it too, because that's the only thing that made sense."

We looked at each other.

I said, "I would like to hug you if you'd let me."

He shook his head as if to say no but then began to lumber forward, his arms outstretched.

We held each other for a long time, then turned to our backyard and readied ourselves to dig the graves.

the chosen of the chosen

It was coming to an end, as we all knew it some day would, the wrath of nature coming to punish the selfishness of man, the conclusion we had all been promised lurking right around the corner. For us nine chosen children the end was solidified by the foretelling of three deaths among our own—how they were chosen we were not sure, two girls and one boy selected from the nine of us, the three children without shadows, the three children slated for death.

On instinct we met near the middle of town so that Olivia, Fredderick, and Michelle could come to us and say goodbye, could kiss our cheeks, could apologize for whatever they might have done to bring the wrath upon themselves, our friends determined to leave us after a quick farewell, promising to stay away from us so as not to include us in their fate. They had each of them awoke without a shadow and noticed right away, as we all, by that point, had been checking ourselves rather frequently, and then they called upon us silently, one by one, to gather together so that we might see each other as a group one final time, in the center of town instead of in the forest so as not to draw suspicion. We of course had to act as if nothing were the matter, as if we were just children gathered to play, and so we mixed in with others, not talking about what would come, or what the rest of us were supposed to do, nothing that we actually wanted to say, but rather just pretending that life was continuing forward, each of us stealing a few moments with our marked friends, pulling them close enough to tell them that we loved them, that we would miss them, and that we would do our best to avenge their deaths.

"Just run," I whispered to Michelle, a girl I had grown very fond of in the previous weeks, slipping my hand into hers as I spoke. "Just pick a direction and start walking, get away from these people. I'll come for you as soon as I can."

"There is no escaping death, honey. Whatever it is, it is meant to happen. I just hope that you and the others will make it through the night."

She kissed my cheek one more time, pulled her hand away, and headed towards the home where she was raised.

first love

That moment with Michelle made me remember my first kiss, back when I was only seven, just moments before my family left the town's winter festival, held that year at the schoolhouse during the first snow of the season. A great deal of our families were there, being social, drinking hot apple cider, letting us be children, allowing us to enjoy a night among our peers, laughing and playing games late into the evening. For the most part we were divided by age, the children ten and under running around and shouting, while the older kids stood in small groups, girls dancing together, giggling, whispering about who they had crushes on, while the boys teased one another and told jokes, acting as if they had no interest in the girls at all. But there was one kid, a girl, a Bethany, then age twelve, who hung out with the younger children, uninterested in the social games played by the kids her age, uninterested in boys, uninterested in gossip. Bethany filled the role of our leader that night, taking it upon herself to be in charge of what games we played, making sure that everyone followed the rules and played fair, keeping score and being the judge when there was any sort of dispute. I found myself drawn to her throughout the evening, always wanting to be by her side, and even became jealous if she spent too much time with another child, forcing myself into these conversations with a joke or a story about myself. Bethany realized, of course, that I had developed a crush on her, and instead of discouraging me away from it she played along, treating me like an equal, allowing me to quit playing the games that she would set into motion and let me help her instead. She asked me a lot of questions as the night went on, and shared a lot about herself, telling me about her older sister and how cold she was, about her father who had left town, and about her mother who would barely speak to her. She seemed okay with things, even optimistic, if only a little anti-social.

"What I like the most is to make things, to be in charge of things, to use my imagination. That's why I like you guys," she said, "because you are all still so interested in ideas."

And then she smiled and I smiled back.

At the end of the night, when the party was winding down, the parents gathering their children to start the walk home through the snow, I became incredibly anxious, afraid to leave the girl, afraid of what would happen when we went out into the night, back into the real world where she was so much older than me, with no similar friends or any reason to spend time together, afraid of a life without her presence.

"I don't want to go home," I said, closer to tears than I thought I was.

She smiled.

"Me neither."

She leaned down and kissed me on the nose.

"Thank you for helping me tonight. If you see me at school you can come say hello. I may not have time to talk, but I'll always say hello."

I hugged her as tightly as I could hold on to a person, then let her go and ran off to my parents, sad and embarrassed about my feelings, but excited that she had touched me.

Bethany kept her promise, always saying hello when we saw each other around school, even walking me partway home from time to time, letting me hug her if I had my courage up enough to try it, but by the next winter festival she was dead and buried, chosen as she was for the sacrifice to harvest, my first kiss lost to the whims of a despicable false prophet and his bloodthirsty followers.

mothers and fathers

I was not there for any of the three deaths, but I could see them in visions, running through my mind just behind my own experience of the moment, in real time as the tragedies unfolded, my close friends struck dead by the people who had once loved them the most.

While I sat down to dinner so did Olivia, obviously worried about her impending death but trying to stay strong, to not let it affect her. She was apprehensive of her food, poking at it, moving it around her plate, hungry but not eating, the idea of dying with food in her stomach sounding wasteful to her.

"Why aren't you eating?" her father asked.

"I'm not hungry."

"Well eat anyway," the man said, a worried tone to his voice, looking at his daughter as if she might stop eating all together and become one of those women made of skin and bones—just sunken eyes, yellow teeth, and stringy hair stuck on top of a stick body, awake forever and driven mad.

"Or what?" she said, her voice determined but a little shaky. "Or else you'll murder me like all those other fathers?"

"Why would you say that?" he asked his daughter, seriously hurt by her accusation.

"Are you going to kill me, father? Are you going to strike me with your hand, or something blunt pulled from a shelf? Are you going to cut me father?" Her voice became a shriek. "Are you going to murder me for not eating my food?"

Olivia took her plate and threw it against the wall, then took her chair and swung it at the man, convinced that he would take it from her and beat her to death with it, but instead he just turned his body to better take the hit.

"Don't say that, pumpkin!" the man said, starting to cry. "I love you!"

In that moment, at the sight of her father crying, Olivia burst into tears herself and ran to the man, wrapping her arms around him.

"I'm sorry father! I've just been so scared!"

"It's okay," he whispered, his eyes closed, rocking his daughter back and forth, his fingers moving through her hair, but then, suddenly, she became heavy in his arms, all of her muscles tightening, and when he opened his eyes and looked at Olivia she looked back with wide, frightened eyes, her mother standing behind her, holding the butcher knife that she had slid mere moments before between two of her daughter's ribs.

"I am your wife," Olivia's mother told her husband. "Not her. Me."

As I was cleaning the kitchen, finishing up the last of my chores before heading to bed, I saw Fredderick sitting alone in his room, looking at his hands, rubbing his fingers together. He seemed fascinated with the mechanics of it, in awe of the control he had over every muscle held within them, amazed that he could move them in such intricate ways with almost no effort at all.

"Son," his father said stepping into the room, blood dripping from his mouth, the coughing having returned for the third time that day, "I need your help gathering some firewood."

Fredderick went to put on his jacket but stopped, not seeing the point, and instead just smiled at his father and walked past him into the hallway. There was a light coming from his parents' room, his mother obviously hidden behind the door, not wanting to see her son leave for the last time.

"Goodnight mom," Fredderick called out. "I'm going to go help dad take care of something outside, and then I'm going to go to sleep. I love you, okay mom? I always will."

And then Fredderick and his father left the house and walked out into the forest, just far enough so that their voices wouldn't carry.

"Father, I forgive you, please, just make it quick."

I saw, just as I was drifting to sleep, Michelle in her own bed, wide awake, waiting to see which of her parents would be bursting in with her bloodshed on their mind, but when the door opened it was her younger sister, Bridgette, age eleven.

"What are you doing in here, honey?"

"I want to sneak out with you."

Michelle smiled, playing dumb.

"Oh, I don't sneak out... You know that."

"You do. I've seen you from my window, you and three others, and I want to go too, or I'll tell mom what you guys do."

"What do we do?" Michelle asked, wondering how much her sister knew about our gatherings.

Bridgette stared blankly and said, "You sneak out..." unsure of what Michelle was looking for, which just made Michelle laugh, not at Bridgette but in relief, the girl positive that she could convince her sister that she was mistaken and send her back to bed, but Bridgette was insulted by the laughter and yelled out for their mother in the kind of high-pitched shriek that only little girls can do.

Before she knew it Michelle's parents were in her room, her sister telling them about her frequent sneaking out, her father's large hands wrapping around her throat, the girl held against the wall, her feet several inches from the ground.

"Tell us the names of the rest of your coven, you little witch!"

She moved her lips but no sound came out, her breath stopped by his strength, so he threw her to the ground and kicked her in the stomach, and in the chest, and in the face.

"Answer your father!" her mother yelled.

"Fredderick..." she said and then was kicked again. "And Olivia."

"There's three!" Bridgette called out, genuinely excited

about what was happening, caught in the moment the same as her parents. "There's another boy! One girl and two boys! She's hiding someone!"

The girls' father lifted Michelle's head and slammed it, hard, against the wooden floorboards.

"Who is this other boy?"

My name, I thought, *say my name, let them kill me so that we can keep the other children safe.*

"I'm sorry," she said, aimed at me I'm sure, but this just angered her father, the man taking his thumb and digging it into her eye as a response.

"Give me a damned name, you devil!"

"His name," she said, "is Timothy," and with that her father snapped her neck with so much force that he nearly pulled her head clear from her shoulders.

I climbed out of bed and got dressed, then sat and waited for the angry mob to arrive and lead me to my death.

a gathering of old friends

I could hear them as they came walking up to my house, calling my name, yelling about spells and hexes that I had supposedly handed out like invitations, hollering about their coming revenge. Within moments they were banging on our front door, demanding that my father hand me over, threatening to kill him along with me if he refused to cooperate. My father came into my room and asked if I knew what they were going on about, willing to hear my side of things before accepting their accusations and throwing me to the savages, but I just nodded back to him, letting him know that I had been expecting this.

"Let them in, father."

He came and kissed me on the forehead, and then went to welcome our guests. My father played along, the man a gifted actor, pretending as if he had been asleep and hadn't heard them approaching, acting shocked when they mentioned my name, then righteously angry when they told him what I had been involved with. He marched the men and women that had come to murder me down the hallway and into my room, but stayed back himself, unwilling to have a real hand in my death. They crowded in, some ten or twelve people, even more in the hallway and in the living room, with several others still arriving outside, carrying things that they had associated with my life, items to be tossed away with my body when they were done with it, but in my room they stayed back from me, unwilling to get close. There was a lot of noise at first, a lot of yelling and name-calling and descriptions of violence, but after a few moments it began to die down until no one was speaking at all, just staring at me with wide, worried eyes.

"Someone grab him," Michelle's father said, but no one came any closer, just stood and stared.

"I can't bring myself to do it," one woman confessed. "I can't bring myself to hurt him."

The room erupted in worried stammering, everyone speaking at once, desperate to try and understand why no one could raise a hand against me, and even more puzzled as to why I was just sitting there, watching them, slightly amused.

"We'll burn down the house!" Carlton exclaimed, a triumphant smile stretching across his face, and the crowd joined him in his elation, relieved that they had come to a solution so quickly. Several men produced matches, but once struck they could not bring themselves to do anything with them, could not touch the flame to the curtains, or to my bed, or to anything else dry and flammable, but would merely stare at the matches, watching them burn down until the heat hit their fingers, then shaking them out, dropping the remains to the floor.

"He's the devil," someone muttered, and then the room was silent once again.

"banished"

It was the symbol, I realized, the one scraped into my thigh keeping me safe, the mark a protection spell, holding back all of the men and women who longed so desperately to harm me. Things had changed very rapidly, the room now genuinely terrified of me, wanting me dead for fear of what I could do to them rather than simply having the urge to kill and looking for any possible excuse, but their eagerness could not bring them any closer to me; did not allow them access to my blood.

I stood and walked towards the crowd to see what might happen, and they parted to let me through, the men and women in the hallway pushing back, unable to get close to me with such hatred in their hearts. I stepped into the living room and then outside to the rest of them gathering at my home, the crowd unaware of what had happened in my room, still angry and yelling about vengeance, foaming at the mouth, ready to tear me to pieces. Suddenly my house went up in flames, the fire catching now that it was no longer a threat to my life, and those inside began to run out in fear, just to see me waiting for them in the yard— some of them ran towards the town, while others rushed back into my house, choosing the fire over a strength that they could not comprehend.

The people outside of the house fell silent, not understanding what was going on. Everyone had gathered together for a lynching, and now there was a house on fire and the boy who should be dead was standing in the grass smiling smugly as the flames devoured the home he had grown up in. Some people left, running scared, but most just lined up and looked at me, a wall of confused faces trying to understand what it was that was keeping them back, all of them muttering about the devil, or about the wolves, or about the ghosts of dead children—all of them, that is, except my father, the man smiling, his eyes wet with tears, obviously proud that I was the one chosen to stop all of this, that I was not marked, as he had been, as a sinner from birth. When he saw my eyes locked on his he smiled wider, showing me his love one final time, and then let a mask of rage take over his face.

"You are the devil!" my father yelled at me. "You are not my son but a beast! I banish you back to nature! Back to your church! Back to where you belong! You have no home here, you devil! You witch! You wicked child!"

He turned to the crowd.

"We can push him back if we have faith! Shout out that you banish him! Cast this devil out! Tell him he has no home here! That he is unwelcome! Reject this wicked spirit and our town will be pure once more!"

They began to shout as my father directed, and I played along, wincing as if in pain, backing towards the woods, letting them think that they were in control of the situation. As soon as I was too far to hit, the crowd began to throw stones, and I yelled out as if they had struck me, as if this was all they had to do for things to return to normal.

home at last

There was a feeling of relief as I retreated into the woods, a weight lifted, as if I were a ship suddenly cut loose from its anchor. I thought of the demons that the men had spoken of, the generational curses that tethered these beasts to men through their tainted blood, those inescapable hardships, those self-fulfilling prophecies of doom, and I imagined a small group of demons, handed down to me from my father, each one with me from birth like a perverse nursemaid, left at the edge of the forest, not actually attached to me but to the town, their tether holding strong. Walking through the woods I felt alive in a way I never had, like a man without a past, and I embraced it, ridding myself of everything I was raised with.

There were good memories among the rest—moments with my mother before she was told to fear me; time spent with my sisters, me in love with both of them in a way that was almost innocent, admiring them from afar; afternoons with my father, the only man I had ever known to look at young men not as children but as future adults, treating every boy that would let him with the utmost respect; and of course the time I spent with the other children when we were left to our own devices, sometimes simple on purpose, other times challenging one another and pushing each other towards adulthood—but I did my best to push those memories away as well, looking forward to whatever it might be that lay hidden behind the trees, tucked away in the darkness that was laid out before me.

three mothers

There were three of them, shoulder to shoulder, their faces hidden in shadow, hovering a few inches off the ground, watching me from behind a few rows of trees. They could not believe their luck—a boy of my age alone in the woods without any effort from them, no mark that they had bestowed, no doubt planted in the minds of the men and women who loved me, a gift from the universe to satisfy their dark desires. They recognized me of course, realized that I was the child who could see them, the one they had tried to lead into the woods alone so many times before, and here I was of my own accord, no weapons in my hands, too far from town to draw any support with my screams for help.

The women smiled behind the shadows they wore like masks, and split from one another to surround me, to close in.

They began to whisper to me, their voices building as they went on, multiplying, coming from a thousand places at once until it was a steady roar of verbiage, of wicked words aimed at breaking me down to the point where I would hand myself over to them, where I would offer my flesh to them like an eager young woman handing herself off to a seasoned older lover.

> "the sun won't help you,
> the moon won't help you,
> love won't help you,
> your gods won't help you
> your father with his belt,
> with his boots and his beard,
> will not be here to help you,
> your tears won't save you,
> your prayers won't save you,
> no promises of a life well lived,
> no apologies for sins committed,
> the salvation you seek is just a myth,
> all you have is us to turn to,
> only our arms to hold you close,
> only our mouths to kiss your face and neck,
> only we can bring relief from the darkness,
> from the agony we will inflict upon you,
> we will be your one true love,
> we will be your everything,
> your mother and father,
> your brother and sister,
> your past and your future,
> and you will be all things to us,

will fulfill our every need,
we will steal and then eat your flesh,
we will drain and then drink your blood,
we will bathe in a river of your tears,
and we will wear your skin like clothing,
replace our bones with yours,
our hair with yours,
our flesh with yours,
staying young and soft
and beautiful until the sun
dies in the sky and
we inherit the earth,
the world bathed in our darkness
for all eternity."

The women were circling around me, moving faster as they got closer, their voices washing over me, but then they stopped spinning, stopped moving completely, and just looked at me.

"I can't get any closer," they said in unison, their voices returned to a whisper.

I watched as they tried to reach out and touch me, to dig their fingers into my flesh, but not one of the three women could raise her hands above her waist, their arms shaking violently by their sides as they fought against the invisible forces keeping them back from me. They began to spin again, circling around and around, but they could not break through, and so they stopped again and just stared at me through the darkness. I watched as these women shook, all of their strength focused on reaching me, unwilling to give up, desperate to conquer me, to pull me apart, to taste my flesh, so enveloped in their desires that they did not see the wolves approaching from all sides, rearing back, ready to leap, and then, just as the wolves jumped, the women's feet touched the soil for the first time in years, their magic momentarily lost, so invested in the moment that their spells pulled away from them and they were merely human once again. The shadows that hid their faces disappeared, and beneath them the women were hideous—thin lips, wrinkled skin, bruised and sunken eyes, with mouths so crooked and crowded that it looked as if there were two rows of teeth—but then their faces were hidden again, this time behind a wash of blood, the wolves on top of them, ripping the awful women to pieces.

the chosen one

We walked together in silence, though it was clear that the
wolves were proud of what they had done, that the death
of the witches was something that they had been looking
forward to for quite some time. There were seven of these
wolves, all with dark black fur made even darker with the
splatter of the women's blood, the animals licking their
teeth as we walked, savoring the taste of their victory over
the three dark mothers.

The wolves knew my name, had been told of me long
ago by Raleigh, and had been waiting in the forest for me
to come to them, for me to help them bring an end to all
of this. The wolves were burdened by the curse, generation
after generation living only to exact revenge, to punish the
children of the children of the children of the men who
killed their goddess, and they longed for it to finally be over

with. They told me I had to go with them, that their goddess was about to return to our realm, coming back to cleanse the valley of its blight and lead the wolves in a hundred years of good fortune, but to do so a son of man must be present, one who is true of heart and respects nature, someone who can bless the wolfmother as she blesses him.

I was not at all certain that I was the young man they were looking for, but with no other option I followed the wolves through the woods and up into the mountain.

the wolfmother is born

There was a smell, sick and sweet all at once, wafting towards us, coming down the mountainside, and then suddenly we were there, a cave dug into the mountain, a den of wolves some fifty strong, with a large beast, nearly the size of a bear, lying on her back in the center of the cave, her legs open, her slit wet and pulsating. The enormous wolf had apparently already gone into labor, was ready to give up her life to bring their goddess into being, and was simply waiting for me, as they had been for generations, to come and say the words that would guide this child out. The wolves that had escorted me dropped down to the ground, their legs tucked beneath them like the rest of their brothers and sisters—just as the wolves had done in our vision—and then nodded for me to approach the birthing wolf.

"It is time."

I walked slowly to the wolf, could feel the heat from between her legs as I approached, the feeling like the warmth of the sun that I had seen so little of in prior months, the heat of new life. I continued up the side of the wolf's body up to her face, looked into her eyes and saw that she had love for me, that she held no grudge for the sins of my parents and their parents before them, but rather cared deeply for me, had been waiting—not just for the words, but for me specifically, for the breath that I would use to carry them. I placed my hand on her forehead, closed my eyes, and let the words flow through me, delivered not from memory but as a gift from some other realm. The great wolf began to tremble, and as I finished the spell I opened my eyes once more to see that she still had her eyes locked on mine, that she was giving me all of her love, even through to her final breath, and then her eyes closed and she was lost to us as a young woman crawled from between her legs, the girl's long hair like an autumn sunset, her pale skin dotted with freckles, her eyes wide and alert, the irises as grey as the winter sky, her pupils as deep as wells, as distant as the ocean floor.

The wolves stood up, one by one, and walked forward to lick their goddess clean.

one slow, sweet kiss, and then gone forever

I stood with her, looking over the forest at the town below, at the fire that continued to burn, smoke pouring into the sky, joining the clouds to help block out the light of the moon. We were both naked, as it felt unnatural to stay clothed in her presence, her beautiful body making me ashamed of my shame, the girl so gorgeous that I felt perfect standing next to her. I grabbed her hand and she let me, squeezing mine when I squeezed hers first, and we stared ahead as she told me what to do, instructed me to guide the children north, to find an area with water, and with fruit, and with birds and rabbits, and to make the place our home.

"We were raised," I said, "worshipping the owls and

cats. How do we worship the wolves? How do we worship you?"

She shook her head, disappointed in me.

"Do not worship me. Do not worship anything," she said

I squeezed her hand and she squeezed mine back.

"I have to go now and cleanse the town. I will send the worthy among the children up the mountain to meet you. Right here, so don't move an inch."

"Will you please spare my father?"

"No," she said, leaning in, kissing me slowly on the mouth. "I won't."

She began to make her way down the mountainside, the wolves walking close behind her, their mouths already frothing, ready to destroy every man and woman that I had ever known—the people who had helped to raise me, who I had held hands with in church, whose tables I had eaten from, whose floors I had slept on in the summers and over winter break—every person who had ever taken me on their knee to tell me a story was about to be struck down by a vengeful woman and her pack of wild dogs.

When the girl was out of sight, lost in the trees, I put my clothes back on and sat down to rest, waiting for the small group of children that I would lead into the darkness, wishing, with all my heart, that I could live with the wolves instead.

About the Artist

Jennifer Parks is a comic artist, illustrator, and co-owner of Pony Club Gallery in Portland, Oregon. Her world is filled with ghosts, charcoal, and ornamental gatherings. Her work tells the tale of that world in intensely rendered darkness.

www.jenniferparks.blogspot.com

About the Author

Riley Michael Parker was raised in a series of trailers spread across southern California. He had a mullet at the age of ten, and a pierced ear, and wore sleeveless t-shirts with skateboarding rats on the front, but he eventually got over all that. He nearly drowned when he was seven, was electrocuted at the age of eleven, and once fell asleep while driving. He is in love with a short and pasty woman, has a cat named Bruce, and can't drink for shit.

Riley is also a writer, a filmmaker, and a visual artist living in the Pacific Northwest. He is the author of the chapbooks OUR BELOVED 26TH and BOYS, and has collaborated on short films with Chelsea Martin and Colleen Rowley, among others. in January 2011 he started a publishing company, HOUSEFIRE, which released its first collection of poems and short stories, the high concept NOUNS OF ASSEMBLAGE, in August of that same year.

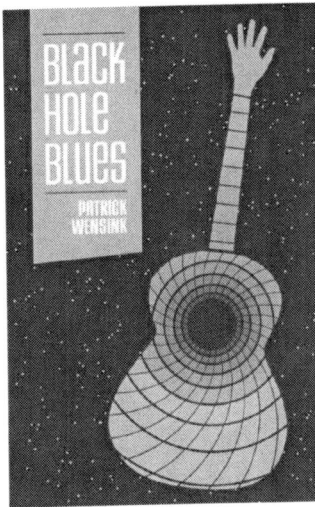

BLACK HOLE BLUES

PATRICK WENSINK

"No one with a function-ing cardiovascular system can read this book without laughing at least twice per page." —PANK

"Raising Arizona meets quantum physics."
—CHICAGO CENTER FOR LITERATURE AND PHOTOGRAPHY

"Wensink has accomplished an incredible feat: using nothing more than his sagacious imagination, he somehow convinced me to give a shit about country music."
—AIN'T IT COOL NEWS

"A page turner...you have no idea what is coming next but you are still so invested in the core of the tale. It is life or death, but there are still moments of humor that are so entertaining. "
—WHAT TO WEAR DURING AN ORANGE ALERT?

"...an outrageous book. Readers who delight in the wild flips of imagination will find an undeniable "Da Vinci Code" of pop art postmodernism in Black Hole Blues."
—LEO WEEKLY

"Irreverent, outrageous, and fearless in his choice of material, Patrick Wensink has a true knack for absurdity."
—JOEY GOEBEL, author of *Torture the Artist*

AVAILABLE AT AMAZON.COM

CPSIA information can be obtained at www.ICGtesting.com
Printed in the USA
BVOW030629200212

283263BV00002B/1/P